A CURSED COURSE

THE WITCH OF HENBANE ISLAND
BOOK 8

POPPY BRIDGEMAN

Ebook ISBN: 978-1-990509-79-7
Paperback ISBN: 978-1-990509-80-3

Cover created by Getcovers

FREE BOOK

Use the QR code to Claim your copy of Magic Will Out when you sign up for my newsletter and follow Cossi as she seeks answers to her past.

1

The meditation tent looked different filled with people—or not filled, I guess, because I only had four students. I'd spent the last two weeks arranging chairs in a welcoming circle, setting up the whiteboard D had procured from the mainland because I kept losing the integrity of the display spell.

Now, the coffee station had enough supplies to caffeinate nervous students through their first day. Watching four actual witches, ones I didn't know personally, navigate the space, I found myself questioning if any amount of coffee would get me through this without completely humiliating myself.

"Deep breath," I muttered, checking my watch. Nine o'clock. Time to start. Time to pretend I knew what I was doing.

"A wise emperor enters battle prepared but calm," Destroyer observed. He was perched on the tent's support beam. I appreciate his offer to observe, even if his comments were always couched in some kind of imperial nonsense.

"It is not nonsense."

"If you don't want me to think it is, don't keep acting like I agree with your plan to take over the world," I said to him without speaking aloud. I know everyone can talk to their familiar, but I was the only one here who had one, and I couldn't shake the feeling I looked crazy talking to a crow. Of course, since I could talk to any animal, it had plenty of chances to look insane.

I turned my attention back to the four students who were settling into their chairs with varying degrees of comfort. I'd read their applications multiple times, memorized their background checks, and prepared what I hoped was a thoughtful introduction of what it meant to be a protector.

What I hadn't prepared for was the reality of being responsible for teaching them anything useful. Let alone how to know when you need protector magic. It's not like the job comes with clear boundaries. A protector did what was needed to keep the magical world safe from threats inside and outside. We couldn't let the plain humans learn we existed, and because we were still human even with magic, we weren't perfect.

"Good morning," I said, trying to project more confidence than I felt. "I'm Cossi Fortuna, and welcome to the first session of protector training. I know this is new territory for all of us—including me, if I'm being honest. But I think that shared experience of learning might actually be an advantage."

The woman sitting closest to the coffee station smiled warmly. She was probably in her early forties, with practical clothes and an air of calm competence that made me immediately envious. Her background was in teaching magical history.

"I'm Magda Potter," she said. "And I have to say, your

honesty is refreshing. I've been teaching long enough to know that the best learning happens when everyone admits they're figuring things out together."

When she shook my hand, I reached out with my emotional reading power—I refused to call it empathic ability because that would mean I cared about what I read —I didn't always, or perhaps I mean I didn't in that way. In Magda, I read genuine warmth, nervous anticipation, and a slight shadow that might be just first-day nerves. Nothing concerning.

"Your background in education will be really valuable here," I said. "I'm hoping we can all learn from each other's different perspectives and experiences."

The man sitting next to Magda stood to introduce himself. He was probably in his mid-thirties, carefully groomed like he came from money and took full advantage of his clothing budget. His smile was practiced but still warm, and when he spoke, his voice had that smooth quality of someone comfortable with public speaking. His emotions were all reflective of his appearance. Smooth, no nerves, no spikes of anything.

"Samuel Whitlock," he said, offering his hand to everyone in the circle. "I'm so excited to finally be here. My family has a long tradition of magical service, and when I realized I might learn to be a protector, I spent months researching the old stories. I noticed the dwindling numbers a while back, but I didn't think there was a solution."

He was genuinely enthusiastic. There was just something about how polished his presentation came across. It made me wonder if he was trying a bit too hard. I put it down to nerves and reminded myself how I tried really hard to fit in when I first arrived. They would all have a bit of anxiety.

"What made you apply?" I asked.

"About six months ago," Samuel said. "There was a situation in my community—someone was using magic to manipulate local decisions. I found myself able to compel them to stop and explain what they'd been doing. Very surprising, but obviously necessary for community protection." He paused, then added with humility, "Though I'm sure I handled it clumsily. That's why I'm here—to learn how to use my abilities as a protector would. Unless you think we'll get protector magic?"

It was exactly the kind of origin story you'd expect from someone who could learn to be a protector. Maybe that's why it felt slightly rehearsed—he'd probably practiced it while he was digging into the past and hoping to get accepted. "We'll find out about the magic through the lessons." I mean, maybe he was right, but I couldn't count on it.

The man sitting across from Samuel had been quiet during the introductions, his attention focused on the chair he was sitting in. I noticed him pressing his palm against the seat, then testing the stability of the frame with small movements. When he realized we were waiting for him, he looked up with an expression that mixed determination and deep sadness.

"Jasper Sturn," he said simply. His voice was quieter than I'd expected. His hands showed old burns and scars from his work at the forge. Metalworkers didn't seem to notice the little wounds. "My wife died four months ago. Accident that could have been prevented if someone with protector training had been there. I don't want that to happen to anyone else."

The grief rolling off him was heavy and complicated—fresh mourning tangled with anger and something harder.

When he gripped the edge of his chair, I saw his knuckles go white. This kind of pain could go in two directions: revenge or repair. He'd taken a step in both directions by the tinges of violet and acid green in his emotions. His choice to apply here meant he'd decided on repair.

"I'm very sorry for your loss," I said gently. "That's a difficult reason to be here, but I understand why you need to take steps to heal."

"People think good intentions matter," Jasper said, and there was an edge to his voice that made me pay attention. "They don't. Competence matters. Results matter. My wife is dead because someone meant well but didn't actually know what they were doing."

The bitterness of those words created an uncomfortable silence. Samuel shifted in his chair and made a small sympathetic sound. Magda's emotions softened with compassion. The other student grasped his shoulder in comfort. Jasper didn't seem comfortable with any of the reactions.

"I hope this course will help. Protectors are scarce but remember our primary job is to ensure the plain humans never learn of our existence," I said. "We all have our personal skills that align with our powers. Not every protector can heal, or create works of art." I suspect my personal skill was investigating, but it wasn't like I'd had time to explore anything other than catching killers.

I let that sink in for a moment before continuing. "When we are needed, I hope we can step up. Perhaps we can honor your wife's memory by making sure the next generation of protectors is prepared. I might be one of the last born to the job, but training will fill that gap. And this first class is going to make sure the lessons work."

Jasper nodded, but I caught the way his jaw clenched.

The anger underneath his grief was raw, and I'd work hard to keep him on the healing side of it.

The fourth student had been taking notes since everyone started talking, his pen moving rapidly across the pages of a well-used field journal. Before he looked up, I could see the excitement flowing from him. No nerves for this student, just eagerness for knowledge and to help.

"Ravi Jain," he said, grinning at the group. "I've been awake since four AM because I'm so excited to be here. I'm an ecologist and Henbane is such a trove of species. Nowhere else I've visited is so biodiverse. The earth witches are doing a fabulous job. I'm hoping to take some of their techniques to other communities. I talked a few this morning. They said they'd be happy to share. Protecting our world is bound to the health of our planet."

If he kept up this level of enthusiasm, he'd be exhausted —or everyone else would.

"What's your specific focus?" Magda asked.

Ravi's expression became more intense. "Mostly when people think of the environment, they tend to blame the human interaction. Factories spewing out pollutants, cars, whatever. It's never about what we witches might be doing. If protector powers can compel people to stop harmful magical practices..." He paused, then added with a slight edge, "The problem with most magical training is it teaches us to work within systems that are already broken. Protecting nature isn't the same as protecting people's feelings about nature."

Samuel made a thoughtful sound. "That's an interesting perspective, though of course we'd need to be careful about the ethics of compelling behavior for environmental rather than direct community protection purposes."

It was a reasonable point, and his tone was educational

rather than dismissive. Even so, I noticed Ravi's shoulders tense slightly. This was going to be an interesting few weeks.

"Some people prioritize bureaucracy over actual protection," Ravi said. "I respect traditional approaches, but we might need more intervention for the environmental threats we're facing."

The words hung in the air for a moment. I filed it away as something to watch—enthusiasm was good, but extremism would be problematic. And discussion might slip into argument too easily.

"Those are the kind of questions we'll be debating," I said, hoping to avoid a first-day battle. "The boundaries of protector authority, the balance between individual freedom and community safety, and how to apply these abilities in different contexts. How we use our own powers for good. We can start with a short tour of Henbane."

2

The students knew each other a little, I hoped. The group arrived on the same boat from Sechelt last night. They'd been transferred to their bikes and led to The Inner Spell just before midnight. So, the first thing on my agenda was to show them Henbane. It was kind of a legend, and up until now, few strangers came to stay. Mostly relatives, or friends who arrived for visits, or one of the famous festivals.

We got on our bikes, and I took them to the Earth Witch Village, which was only a few minutes ride. Then off to town —okay, it was a main street, not a town—where I introduced them to Jan and Zoe, who were supplying our meals. Mark, as my friend, not as the cop they should be a bit afraid of. Lilibeth, in case they were hoping for a familiar. D as a contact for any technology issues. Lance, who was still running the bookstore. The solitaries wouldn't appreciate a visit, and the Shifter Village was a bit too far this trip.

I missed living above the bookstore. I'd switched homes with Zinnia a month ago because it was clear my presence was needed on site rather than a fifteen-minute ride away.

She wasn't home when we arrived, but I told them about her and the role she played since moving to Henbane. The woman had organizational skills beyond anything I'd seen before.

"This is beautifully designed," Samuel said when we returned to The Inner Spell. His appreciation seemed genuine, but I didn't think a few tents, chalets, and a main building warranted the description. Then, I had no idea what any of their homes were like. In the middle of plain humans, I imagine secrecy was more of a priority.

"You've really thought about creating a space where people feel safe to explore these abilities," he said, gesturing to the tents. "It gives off a feeling of innovation and hope that I've never experienced before."

It was kind of him to say, though he was trying too hard to be the model student. But I was probably being paranoid. Not everyone was Phillip, secretly using hexes to manipulate people while hiding darker intentions. One day, his betrayal wouldn't be so prominent in my mind—I could only hope.

As we walked between tents, I caught sight of Destroyer, his black eyes tracking our movement with an imperial assessment of new subjects. He'd been silent, and it was odd. I was so used to his running commentary.

"Is that your familiar?" Samuel asked, following my gaze.

"That's Destroyer," I said. "He has opinions about everything. Including being the emperor of the world."

"It is who I am," Destroyer announced. I'm sure he hoped I would pass on the words. When I didn't, he continued, "I am simply ensuring these recruits understand proper protocol."

I decided a little levity was in order, so I repeated what

he'd said, all of it. Ravi laughed. "I love that. I wish I had a familiar. It's sometimes lonely in my profession."

"You might get one here," I said. "We always have a few animals approach witches during festivals."

We settled back into the discussion tent, and I launched into what I'd prepared about protector powers. How my powers hadn't changed, I still understood any language— not just human ones—read emotions and could nudge people on a path. What happened when we recognized my status as a protector was subtle.

"Now there's strength when I use them to protect the community," I said. "Yes, there are different powers but that's what we hope to do here. Work with your innate magic to add some of the protector levels. I'm not really sure how. We'll walk that path together."

"What if it doesn't work," Ravi asked. "If it's just a learned thing, anyone could become a protector. Or a healer, or anything really, right?"

"I hope we find a way. I recently met a woman who had none of the usual investigation powers but managed to fill the role quiet well. The other witches are going to help us, so we're not on our own. The most important thing to understand," I said, "is that protector abilities come with limitations and safeguards. The power itself resists being used for personal gain or manipulation. It has to be genuinely about community protection."

"What happens if someone tries to use it for personal purposes?" Magda asked. "I think we need to hear the downside too."

"The powers don't work," I said. "That was my test, and I'll tell the whole story later. But until I used the power as a protector, I couldn't force the truth. I don't know what might have happened if I pushed harder. But we won't go that far.

If it doesn't work, we'll pivot and go at the problem in different ways."

"Can the power be corrupted over time?" Samuel asked. "I've read about witches being twisted by long-term misuse."

I thought about Phillip again. About how his magic had been used to hide crimes and manipulate other innocent witches for years. How the curse rebounded when I removed the hexes.

"Yes," I said. "It's one of the reasons we made this training focus so heavily on ethics and self-reflection. The powers have safeguards, but they work best when you understand and respect them. Like any other magic, evil returns evil."

"Sometimes good intention isn't enough," Jasper said quietly. "You have to actually be competent."

I didn't know how to ease his pain. Doc Rene wouldn't treat him without his consent. If he was stuck repeating that competence statement, how would he move forward to carry her death without so much resentment?

"ALL RIGHT," I said, after an hour of discussion. I was feeling relieved we'd made it through without any major disasters. "I think that's enough theory for today. Tomorrow we'll start with some practical exercises to help you recognize whether you actually have protector abilities that haven't revealed themselves yet. If that's the case, we'll work out what form they take."

"How will we know?" Ravi asked eagerly, leaning forward in his chair. "Or is this something that changes slowly?"

"I imagine it will take some time," I said. "My experience isn't much help because I didn't know I was a witch for most of my life. In less than three months I was a protector. Don't worry, I'm sure once we've done some exercises, we'll talk about how different it feels."

As the students gathered their various papers and discarded sweaters, I felt cautiously optimistic. Despite their differences in powers and experiences, they'd meshed. The discussions revealed more commonality in their outlooks than disagreements. My ability to read the emotions around them told me there was nothing hidden. Or rather, nothing important to the lessons held behind normal shields.

"Don't forget we're going to The Howling Place for dinner. You'll love Sheena's food, and it's just outside the shifter village."

Samuel lingered as the others headed toward the path back to the main building. "Thank you for today," he said. "I know starting a new program like this must be stressful, but you handled it beautifully. If there's any way I can help—administrative work, research support, whatever you need—please don't hesitate to ask."

It was a nice offer, though something about the eagerness made me slightly uncomfortable. I pushed that thought away. Samuel was clearly someone who wanted to make a good impression and be useful. That wasn't a crime.

"I appreciate that," I said. "Let's see how the practical work goes tomorrow."

After everyone left, I sat alone in the meditation tent with Destroyer, reviewing the day and trying to quiet my anxious brain. Still a little too keyed up to try for a trance state.

"The new recruits show promise," Destroyer observed, preening his feathers. "Though maintaining order will require imperial oversight."

"What did you really think of them?" I asked. "Any concerns?"

"The female with teaching experience understands proper respect for authority," he said. "The metalworker carries weight of loss that could become problematic. The young one with excessive enthusiasm needs guidance on appropriate channels for passion. The helpful one is very correct in all his behaviors."

That last observation made me pause. "Very correct?"

"As a wise emperor notes when subjects perform expected roles with the appropriate respect," Destroyer said. "Whether respect indicates genuine nature or careful study remains to be determined. It may not matter either way."

I thought about Samuel's polished responses, his perfect student behavior, his seemingly genuine but slightly rehearsed charm. Was I just uncomfortable because I didn't like to be praised? "I'm overthinking this," I said out loud. "First day jitters for everyone—including me. They all seem like good people who want to learn and serve their communities. I need to stop looking for problems everywhere."

"A wise emperor prepares for all contingencies while hoping for the best," Destroyer replied.

"That's surprisingly balanced advice."

"As the emperor, I contain multitudes." He fluffed his wings in pride.

One day I'd figure how a bird who couldn't read came up with quotes like that.

"Any chance you know if the students will get familiars?" If they paired with animals, I could get Destroyer involved as a conduit between the humans and the familiars.

"I am not interested in matchmaking," he cawed before cocking his head and then taking flight.

I locked up the training facilities and walked up the path

to the main building, trying to focus on what had gone right rather than my paranoid tendency to look for problems. The program had launched successfully. Four engaged students were ready to learn. I had support from Mrs. V, Mark, and D if anything went wrong. Lilibeth would tell me if any familiars came knocking.

The first day was done. I'd survived it. That was enough.

3

W e'd managed to get ourselves organized and on the way to Sheena's bar in plenty of time to arrive before dark. "The solitaries all live over in that direction," I pointed out as we made the turn from the main road. The four visitor bikes were painted a pretty yellow, with symbols for peace and safety added in deep purple script. Beulah looked as adorable as usual with my latest addition of a new gel seat.

"Will we tour their area?" Magda asked. "I've never met a solitary witch. On the mainland they generally retreat a long way from the towns."

"I've arranged a few lessons with Jeffery, and Azalea. Both are solitary and their research covers a good part of the world, so they should have some interesting insights."

I put Beulah in the small parking area and waited until the students did the same. Tonight would be about bringing them into a team. No training, no discussions of future problems. Right now, I thought of them as students, a little variation in their powers and outlooks. They saw each other as strangers, and I'd noticed a little rivalry with Samuel—probably what was behind his teacher's pet antics.

By tomorrow morning, we would be people to each other.

Sheena waved us to a table in the corner, a little privacy, but not too far from other customers. Lance was behind the bar, still working here when the bookstore was closed. His beer and cider clubs were still very popular.

Sheena wandered over to our table as soon as we settled. Like all the shifters, she was beautiful. Like a goddess of hearth and home, with a big dollop of sex kitten.

"I've come up with a welcome menu," she said. "Let me know if you want anything different. You can drink what you want, I'll get the boys to take you home if you get too happy. Or, I have some sober up tea."

I wouldn't be getting drunk tonight, but I appreciated not having to make the arrangements if any of my guests decided to overdo it.

"I'm happy to take your recommendation," Magda said. "I'll make sure to leave room for everything."

"Fine with me," Samuel said. "Anyone have allergies? Food preferences?"

"Don't like gamey meat," Jasper said. "I'm okay with what you planned."

I saw the flash of offense in Sheena's emotions. She would never serve anything gamey-tasting. She didn't say anything, and the emotion died out.

"And you, Ravi, right?"

"Is it exclusively Henbane ingredients? I'm looking forward to tasting the difference."

"Some of the spices come in. The earth witches do have some limitations. I only use off-Island supplies when we don't have something." She waved behind her for Lance to bring the beers. "The food will start coming out in a few minutes. It's family style. Enjoy."

I waited until we all had drinks before starting my excellent plan of getting to know them.

"They should obey you as my emissary," Destroyer said.

"Thanks," I said before asking him to let me focus for the evening.

"I'm, not sure what you really know about me," I said. "Is there anything you want to clear up before we get into the lessons?"

"You are the witch who solved a decades long mystery," Ravi said. "Cleared so many hexes without becoming ill."

"You grew up on the mainland. Your witch nature was suppressed," Jasper added. I was glad to see him join in. It might be the beer, but maybe he was getting past his grief.

I nodded at each statement and looked at Samuel. "All true, what about you, Samuel. Any questions?"

"I'd love to know how it felt to become a protector," he said. "You could be the only one who would notice. Growing up without magic."

"Why don't you tell us a story about how you came here," Magda asked.

I hoped her empathy powers were telling her to help me. Otherwise, she was reading my mind, and that was not possible.

Lance brought the plates and bowls of our meals. "More beer? Or would you like some cider?"

I didn't want them falling down drunk, but a little alcohol might serve my purpose. "His cider is incredible. Why don't we get a round of that and then we'll decide how much more we want."

He returned with the pints and said to wave if we needed refills.

"So your story," Samuel said, digging into the bowl of stew to ladle out a serving.

"It's a bit embarrassing, if I'm honest." I thought back to that day when I read dad's letter and cast the spell. "My dad passed away and left me a letter. That's how I learned what they'd done to my powers. Now, let's be clear, I was not a teenager, but I acted like one. He told me not to come here, but I answered Phillip's invitation."

"No one likes to have their life turned upside down," Magda said. "I'm sorry about your parents."

"Thanks. I guess we know that my dad didn't want Phillip to have any control of me. But he was under one of those hexes, I guess and couldn't write the details because it would kill him."

"Perhaps the protector power was already working," Samuel said. "If you chose another community, Raziel would still be corrupting the magic."

I'd figured that out months ago. "Whatever made me come, I'm thankful. I fit here."

"You don't grieve?" Jasper asked. He'd barely touched his food. "I didn't mean that to sound judgmental, but..."

"I miss my parents a lot," I said. "They would be unhappy if I couldn't move on. My mom died when I was really young. Then my dad when I was almost independent."

"Why don't you tell us about your wife," Magda asked. Like she was in on the whole plan. "Her name was Charlotte, right?"

He looked down at his glass. I waited because he was fighting the urge to close down. Magda and I were probably the only ones who knew that.

Finally, he looked up at us. "We met at a spring fair. Her family was selling charms and teas. I knew as soon as I saw her that she would be my life. Like I'd only seen the world through a screen before."

He paused to wipe his eyes.

"Not many witches find their other half," Ravi said.

"It's a curse when one of you dies," Jasper said. "We were married within six months. Someone else tell their story."

I sat back and ate. We had all night and I didn't want this to feel like some kind of investigation. The food was perfect as usual. Warm sourdough bread, stewed beef, fresh vegetables and baked potatoes. Sure it was a bit heavy, but magic burned calories and shifters needed a lot of fuel.

"Let's lighten it up a bit," Ravi said. "This meal deserves fun. I was on field work a year ago, I can't believe it was that long now I say it. This was in the plain world because they do so many more team projects. They find more information faster than a single witch can. So, you know how hard it can be to hide your magic, right."

He paused to let someone agree, but we were all waiting for the actual story.

"So, we were in Ontario looking for evidence that a logging operation was destroying habitat for a bat colony. You know they keep the mosquitoes in check, right?"

He took a drink. Why did I feel like this was a long, winding set up for a joke?

"So, it's evening, that's when the bats hunt so easier to find their caves. The plain humans were poking around. You know how they can be. Get an idea in their heads and they get blind to anything else."

"It's quite annoying," Samuel said. "I've worked with that kind, and the other end of the spectrum. Plain humans who can't focus for five minutes in a row."

"I tried to warn them, but they stumbled into a clump of poison sumac. How they missed the signs I have no idea.

One of them fell face first. I had to go in and save them, because everyone else was just complaining."

"How is that funny?" Jasper asked.

"I suppose funny is in the eye of the beholder. But, I had to come up with a long explanation of why I wasn't affected. I mean, it's a pretty easy spell, and one you can do without a big production. I wanted to heal them all, but can you imagine what would happen? So I made an old family recipe in a salve that night and minimized the damage." He put air quotes around the words old family recipe.

I focused on his actions. He'd used magic around plain humans. Was that common? Wouldn't that risk exposing us? I asked him.

"We do it all the time," Magda said. "Nothing that will raise suspicions. But you must know plain humans are willing to try any homeopathic medicine these days. Most of it is some kind of scam, but we can't not help. If someone is in pain, I can't walk away. I'm sure Ravi felt the same."

Samuel finished his bowl and waved for cider refills. "Your magic suppression likely took that urge away. But we live among them and like Magda said, it's kind of impossible to turn away."

I thought again about how we didn't have any guidelines for staying hidden. Perhaps we didn't need them.

Lance took our empty plates when he delivered the fresh drinks.

"It's harder for witches with my powers," Magda said. "We often go into fields like counseling to give us an outlet. Not using healing magic, but knowing exactly what the patient is feeling, or needs, means we're successful. I had a patient once who thought she was possessed. Dreams and a few hallucinations sent her to a doctor. They prescribed meds for schizophrenia. I found a tiny kink in her aura. She had a tumor. She convinced her doctor to look and today she's healthy. I could have dealt with it myself, but she'd spend her life on meds she didn't need."

"You heal too?" Samuel asked.

"Somethings not everything." Magda took a sip of her drink. "It's too complicated. I'd was terrified I'd attract a cult following. It's bad enough to let a patient walk away without telling them the real cause of their problems. I keep so many secrets. I came here to find another path."

A plate of pastries arrived on our table, giving me a reprieve from the stories. I understood Magda's motives. Changing her career to protector took the plain humans out of the picture, but protector wasn't a career choice. A good topic for a lesson.

"I imagine plain human counselors have the same problem," Samuel said. "I haven't had the same experience. I worked with witches exclusively. No secrets to put me in harm's way."

An odd way to put it. Why would keeping a secret no one knew you had be harmful?

"I suppose I'm the last one to tell my story. I'll keep it short because I can't be the only one who needs to rest."

"True," Jasper said. "This meal, delicious as it was, is adding to my fatigue."

"Then I'll just say my work in service of the community is what brought me here. I cannot share any of the details because I swore to keep promises. But there was a funny incident when I was about ten. I was schooled privately, as you probably know. I had three tutors and my favorite game was eluding them. I found a spell, my parents should have guarded their library better, it allowed me to cast an illusion on myself. I became the image of one of the cooks. All the time my tutors rushed around casting spells to track me, I was watching. Of course I couldn't hold the spell for very long, and I was caught out."

Funny seemed to have a very different meaning for witches on the mainland. "Let's head back. Tomorrow you'll need to be rested and alert."

4

The second day started with coffee and cautious optimism. I'd arrived at the training facility early to set up for our first practical exercise—a simple meditation designed to help students recognize the subtle difference between ordinary powers and the specific feel that accompanied protector abilities. Something I should have asked Mrs. V. When my protector powers woke, it felt like something uncurling from a nap in my core. Perhaps it was different for her.

"You are making a noise," Destroyer observed from the tent's center pole. "What does that mean for our imperial plans."

"I'm humming. It means I'm in a good mood?" I asked, arranging cushions in a circle. I wondered how this was the first time I'd done that.

"The wise emperor knows that good moods in the face of uncertainty are merely optimism wearing a disguise." He ruffled his feathers. "We deal in reality."

He lived in a delusion. I cut that thought before he could take offense. "You're very philosophical this morning."

"I am a complex emperor." He swooped from the tent like he was impersonating an owl.

The students arrived together. It made sense. They were staying in the main room, and there wasn't much time for them to dawdle in the short walk down the path.

Ravi was talking enthusiastically about something involving ecosystem magical signatures while Jasper listened with polite attention. Samuel carried a tray of pastries he'd picked up from the buffet Zoe left us.

"I thought everyone might appreciate a snack later," Samuel said, setting the tray on the small table near the coffee station. "Meditation can be quite a strenuous mental exercise. And every meal I've had so far is delightful. Like the ideal version of whatever it is."

He was right on the mark. From Zoe's simple grilled cheese sandwich to the inventive modern food at the bistro, each bite was perfect. Bringing the treats was thoughtful of him. After a meditation a bit of sweetness helped perk up the participants.

Magda helped him set the tray on the side table. I'd put focus tea ready and later we'd have coffee. I wanted people calm to start the session, so caffeine was off the list until we finished the meditation.

"This is exactly what I was hoping for," Magda said warmly. "Such a small group supporting each other. I've experienced the opposite, where the students became competitive. Not the best way for long-term training."

We settled into the circle, and I guided them through the basic meditation exercise. It was simple—focusing attention on the sensation of wanting to protect something or some-one, then noticing what that felt like in the body and mind.

The quiet of our surroundings helped keep the distrac-tions down. For the students at least. I couldn't help hearing the little conversations going around us. Squirrels, sparrows, other land creatures going about their everyday gossiping. Good thing my job was to lead, not to join them. As they progressed, I used my power to read their emotional state.

Ravi seemed completely absorbed in the exercise, his breathing steady and focused. Jasper sat very still, eyes closed, jaw clenched in what I hoped was concentration but was likely something else. This was not the time to pry. Samuel radiated relaxation and attentiveness, following the instructions perfectly. Magda's face showed deep concentration, and I caught occasional flickers of discomfort crossing her features. My powers told me more was going on beneath the physical, but I let it go.

After twenty minutes, I brought them back to regular awareness. "How did that feel?" I asked.

"Interesting," Ravi said immediately. "There was this moment where the focus felt different—almost like touching something solid in my mind that I hadn't known was there."

"That's a good description," I said, pleased. "That sensation of touching something that already exists rather than creating something new is a good sign." Perhaps we'd attracted actual protectors who simply needed awakening.

"I felt something similar," Samuel said. "Though I wasn't sure if I was actually experiencing the power or just imagining it based on your description."

That was honest, and a bit surprising from him. I appreciated the self-awareness rather than the sucking up.

Magda nodded at the others. "I had that same question. It's hard to know if what you're experiencing is real or just wishful thinking."

"That's exactly why we practice," I said, grateful she'd asked. I didn't want to just lecture them. This was an exercise in discovery, after all. "Over time, you'll develop confidence in recognizing the difference. Jasper, how was it for you?"

Jasper opened his eyes slowly. "I felt angry," he said bluntly. "The whole exercise, all I could think about was my wife dying because someone wasn't competent enough to protect her. I don't know if that's the power or just... grief."

The raw emotion in his voice made everyone shift uncomfortably. Samuel looked sympathetic but slightly uncertain how to respond. Ravi reached over and patted Jasper's shoulder briefly. Magda hid it well, but I could see her need to comfort someone so wounded.

"Grief can definitely affect how we experience these exercises," I said, hoping I was right. "And anger about injustice or preventable harm can actually be connected to protector instincts—the desire to prevent future harm. But we'll need to work on separating the emotion from the ability, so you can use the power effectively without being driven by trauma."

I wasn't sure where all this was coming from. I didn't feel the protector power inserting itself. Maybe I learned more than I thought while getting my marketing degree.

Jasper nodded, but I noticed his hands gripping his knees hard enough that his knuckles had gone white. I couldn't let his pain block his chance at succeeding, but I'd leave dealing with it to our private sessions.

"I think that's a good place to stop for this morning," I said, checking the time. "I've left you time to wander the island on your own. Henbane is such an unusual place, perhaps without plain humans around, you can be free to explore more than just the physical."

I needed time to myself as well, but it sounded selfish to

say so. I'd brought them here, I should keep my focus on the students, right?

"I'd love to stay and help set up," Samuel said. "If you need any assistance, please don't hesitate. I am here to learn not sightsee."

Way to make your colleagues look bad.

"That's okay," I said. "I need to review my notes anyway. We'll reconvene at two. That should give you time to learn about the local area and grab something to eat."

He looked hurt by my refusal of help. I'd been kind about it. If he needed more validation, I might have to rethink his suitability. His emotions were all surface, anything deeper hid behind a glossy shield. He was entitled to his privacy, for now, but holding himself apart wasn't healthy.

The three men hurried away, separating on the main road to their own interests. Magda loitered outside the tent entrance. "Could I talk to you for a minute?" she asked.

"Of course," I said, gesturing to the chairs and hiding my impatience to leave. "What's on your mind?"

Magda glanced toward the trail where the others had disappeared, then back at me. "This is probably nothing, but during the meditation, I kept getting these... surges of discomfort. Like my empathic abilities were picking up something wrong, but I couldn't pinpoint what or where it was coming from. And I started to worry my empathy might be a barrier to success."

Why would she think that? Empathy was a huge asset for any witch. "I think empathy is a benefit not a detriment. But we'll know more as we proceed." I couldn't ignore her sense that something was off. Our powers were similar, but mine just read the emotion. I didn't feel anything about what I learned—no more than a plain human would, anyway. "Explain the feeling off part."

"I don't know exactly," she said, pressing her fingers to her temples. "It's hard to describe. Like someone was working very hard to project the right image, but underneath there was something else. Or maybe I'm just overwhelmed by being around new people with strong emotions. Witches who are free from the anxiety of living among the plain. Yesterday was a lot of new stimuli for empathic abilities."

Was this about Jasper's pain? I didn't think he was putting on a different image, just the opposite. "Do you think it's something to be concerned about?" I asked.

Magda shook her head, though she looked uncertain. "Probably not. I think I'm just tired and processing a lot of new information. The meditation was intense, and I've got this headache that won't quit." She smiled and patted my arm as if I was the one who needed assurance. "I'm going to grab lunch and maybe lie down for an hour before the afternoon session. That'll probably help. There are plenty of opportunities for me to explore later."

"Sounds like the right thing," I said. "But if you continue feeling uncomfortable or if the overwhelm gets worse, please let me know. I can adjust the exercises, or we can work on shielding techniques. I can call on Doc Rene to heal you."

"I appreciate that," she said, standing to go. "I'm sure it's fine."

After she left, I sat in the tent for a few minutes, trying to decide if I should be concerned. Her emotions as I read them were confused, but not alarmed. She was an adult, not a child needing help. Was I looking for problems where none existed?

Maybe not. The way she told me someone was working hard to project the right emotional responses made me think of Phillip. How he'd done just that for decades. Had stolen Elias's emotions to cover the lack of his own. Until I remembered he was the only witch who'd been so horrible, I'd wait for something more concrete before acting. Paranoia didn't help me make good choices.

"Your instincts are always right," Destroyer said. Then before I accepted the compliment he added, "As my witch you cannot be wrong. Unless you disagree with me."

"I can. People are fallible."

"A wise emperor notes that all humans are to some degree," Destroyer said. "I will send my spy network to observe and report."

"That's not particularly reassuring." I imagined an invasion of small animals and birds that would disrupt our lives.

"They will be discreet or face imperial wrath."

I got the feeling he was hoping to wield his powers in a less than benevolent despot way.

"Of course, if no one revolts, being the Emperor of All is quite boring."

5

I decided to spend the break reviewing my afternoon lesson plans rather than dwelling on vague concerns about student dynamics. Mrs. V had warned me that teaching might make me hyper-vigilant about every small issue, and I needed to resist the urge to see problems everywhere—or at least accept that they weren't mine to solve. Tucked into my suite in the main building made it less likely someone would interrupt me.

After a peaceful hour, I headed back to the training facility to set up for the afternoon session. The practical skills tent looked good—I'd arranged stations with different scenarios written on cards, each one presenting a situation where protector authority might or might not be appropriate to use. The students would explain their solution and as a group, we'd discuss it.

The tent was ready—okay, I'd set it up perfectly and I was really just soothing my anxiety by checking. I heard voices in the meditation tent and headed there to remind the students about the change in venue. I got to the entrance and came to a stop.

Magda was lying on the floor near the meditation cushions, her body positioned as if she'd simply decided to lie down during another exercise. But she wasn't breathing, and I couldn't read any emotions from her.

I dropped to my knees, reaching for her wrist to check for a pulse even though some part of me already knew I wouldn't find one.

"No," I whispered. "No, no, no."

My hands were shaking as I pulled out my phone and dialed Mark's number. He answered on the second ring.

"Mark, I need you at the training facility right now. And Mrs. V. And—" My voice cracked. "We need Doc Rene. Magda Potter is dead."

"Are you sure she's gone?" he asked. "Sorry, of course you are."

"I found her body. It looks like—" I forced myself to examine the scene more carefully, shifting into detective mode with no conscious effort. "There's nothing in the tent that would explain what happened. I don't think this was an accident."

"You know the drill. Don't touch anything else," Mark said, and I could hear him already moving. "I'm five minutes away. Keep the scene secure and don't let anyone else in."

"The other students are supposed to arrive for afternoon session in a few minutes," I said. Who had I heard talking?

"Tell them training is postponed. Don't tell them why yet —just that something's come up. I'll be there as soon as I can."

I made the calls with shaking hands. Samuel answered immediately and offered to help with whatever emergency had come up. Ravi sounded disappointed but understanding. Jasper's phone went to voicemail, so I left a message. Why was I acting like this was the first body I found?

Because I might have brought the victim and killer together? Or because I was hoping that this training would be smooth and successful. How was that going to be the case now?

"You are not at fault," Destroyer said. "Do not take on blame you have not earned. It is tarnishing my image."

I ignored him. Yes, he was right, acting this way wasn't going to find the killer, or train my students. My first protector student was dead less than twenty-four hours after the program started. I couldn't let the guilt get in the way, but feeling guilty and letting it get in the way were two different things. Suppressing any emotion was dangerous.

I looked around the room as I waited. Nothing disturbed except for the remaining pastries. Some rodent had come in and taken bites before attempting to carry away a rather tasty looking muffin. We were in the forest, and we'd left food in the open. I doubted the treat thief was involved in the murder, but perhaps we had a witness.

Mark arrived in less than five minutes, Roy at his heels. He took one look at the scene and his expression shifted into the cold professional mask of a cop.

"Tell me exactly what happened," he said, pulling out his notebook.

I walked him through the morning—the meditation exercise, the students' responses, Magda's concern about empathic overwhelm and her headache. My voice stayed mostly steady until I got to the part about finding her body, and then I had to stop and breathe for a moment.

"Did you see anyone else near the tents?" Mark asked.

"No. I was in the practical tent setting up for this afternoon. I heard voices and came to remind whoever it was that we were moving to another tent. I didn't see anyone here, or leaving. But it's a tent, easy to slip out. I'll ask some of the animals when we're done here."

"Not yet," he said. "Let me get my bearings." He moved around the scene, examining everything without touching.

Roy sniffed the air and whined softly. "Tell him I can't separate the traces."

Mark couldn't talk to his dog, no more than a plain K9 officer could. I passed on Roy's comments.

"We might be able to sort something out later," Mark said with a nod to Roy.

Mrs. V arrived next, taking in the situation with one sharp look. She pulled several bottles from her bag and began casting detection spells, her face growing grimmer with each result. I couldn't help thinking it was disappointment in me and not her magic.

"These spells are less helpful that I hoped," she said. "I made them to help Mark or you, Cossi. In case we had another death. All I can tell you is there was no extended violence involved. That someone has laid a powerful confusion spell."

When we'd solved the last murder Phillip committed, Mrs. V spent months researching and developing spells to speed up investigations. Things I might be able to use in the wider world. I mean the only two times I worked with other communities, included murder. She worked with the solitaries to deepen her knowledge, but this was the first time anyone used them. I'd hoped they would always stay untested.

Doc Rene arrived and began her examination, confirming what I think we'd all expected. Magda had been killed approximately two hours ago—which meant sometime shortly after our conversation.

"She came back here," I said, trying to reconstruct what must have happened. "Maybe to practice more on her own, or to try to identify what was causing her discomfort during the group meditation."

"And someone was waiting for her," Mark finished grimly. "Or followed her here. I know we've been surprised before, Cossi, but you've got three suspects here. Three strangers."

"We worked so hard to vet them," I said. Even so, strangers were better suspects than Henbane residents. People we all knew and respected.

"Not for murder," Mark said. "Unless you added a test?"

Mrs. V was already cleaning up the residue of her spells. "I'm afraid we need to shut this program down immediately. It's not safe. I know we need protectors, but not like this."

"No," I said, surprising myself with the firmness in my voice. "What we need is to keep the remaining students together and protect them while we figure out who did this. And I will keep training them."

"Cossi—" Mrs. V threw me her glare of annoyance—I'd seen it plenty throughout my training.

"If we shut down the training, how will we keep the suspects together?" I asked. "I can't ignore the feeling we need to keep going." I'd never had my power push me like this, but I'd follow the urge to protect my students.

Mark was nodding. "She's right. We need to contain this. Keep the investigation close and the suspects where we can watch them. If it's not one of them, we'll be looking at all the residents soon enough."

Surprise leaked through her usually solid shields. I guess no one usually argued with her.

"I don't like it, but I won't fight you." She dropped the walls around her emotions and stared at me as if daring me to read them.

I wouldn't tell anyone what I saw. She was feeling the

passing of her role. For many decades, Mrs. V had been kind of the head of the protectors. I didn't want to take that away from her, but she'd basically handed it over. I nodded at her in acknowledgment. I wanted to hug her, but valued my life more than that.

She rode away after telling Mark to send any evidence as soon as he found it. Then I waited while Doc Rene called for a couple of shifters to move Magda to her clinic. Mark reached out to D who would set up a murder database.

I sent a call out to the local animals for any information they might have. It would take a while for anyone to answer at this time of day. That left me with only one thing to fret over. How to teach three witches about what it took to be a protector while suspecting one of them of murder.

"First lesson in protector work," I muttered to Destroyer. "Apparently it's how to investigate murder while main-taining professional boundaries with your suspects. I don't know when I became a detective but this couldn't be what protectors normally do."

"A wise emperor learns through adversity," Destroyer said.

"Not helping."

"Truth rarely does."

When Mark finished his calls, he came over to where I was standing. "Are you sure about this? Continuing the program?"

"No," I said honestly. "But I'm sure that stopping it won't help us catch whoever killed Magda. And I think she'd want us to make sure this didn't happen to anyone else. If one of them is killer, that means two are still potential protectors."

Mark nodded. "Then I'll get D doing deeper background checks. And we'll need to interview all three remaining students. I want to establish timelines and figure out who had the best opportunity and strongest motive. And who was here talking to Magda after she was murdered. Right?"

"I didn't make that connection," I said. "I keep forgetting about the voices. Maybe one voice? But yeah, Magda was long dead at that point."

I thought about her comment this morning—about someone working to project the right emotional responses while hiding something underneath. She'd sensed the danger. Had her perceptiveness gotten her killed?

6

W e decided to meet at Mrs. V's to sort out our next steps. Away from our suspects who still didn't know Magda was dead. I'd left the remaining students with Jeffery, a solitary with wonderful curiosity and research powers. He would keep them busy until I got back.

Mrs. V's cottage was the best place to meet because of her library, secret storage room, and collection of ingredients. It was also the home of her familiar, Tulip. A now fully grown lynx with the attitude of a godfather—and I don't mean the kindly one who gives you candy. She stretched out in the corner and watched us like we were about to offend her sensibilities.

D joined us a few minutes after I arrived, his laptop sat open on the counter ready to share all the details.

"This is the background checks on all three students," he said without preamble. "More than what we did to qualify them. I'm pulling everything—social media, public records, magical community registrations, educational history, everything. Technology is faster than magic for this stuff."

"I left wards around your retreat," Mrs. V added. "Just to tell us when people come and go." She nodded toward the boiling kettle. I took the hint and made tea.

Mark had his notebook open. "Doc Rene is completing the full examination now. She'll have preliminary findings within the hour."

I sat at the table feeling simultaneously grateful for their immediate mobilization and guilty about pulling them into another murder investigation. "I'm sorry," I said. "This was supposed to be a simple training program."

"Don't take on the guilt," Mrs. V said, echoing Destroyer's words. "You did what was necessary. You are not responsible for the shortage of protectors, or the crime committed."

"She's right, Cossi," D said as he typed a search request. "Nothing in their backgrounds gives me a hint even knowing one of them might be a killer. According to their applications, Samuel comes from a family tradition focused on community service. Jasper's a metalworker with no formal education beyond basic training all kids get. Ravi's background is environmental studies at a mundane university. It's not unusual. I went to UBC for my tech degree."

"Someone did a good job covering," Mark said his voice flat. "We weren't looking for criminal potential, just magical and attitude."

"I imagine each of them had secrets," Mrs. V pointed out. "You had your pick of hundreds of applicants. These four did something to stand out, so you chose them."

Mark's phone alerted with a text. "Doc Rene," he said before turning his phone for us to read. *Preliminary findings ready. Coming to you.*

It didn't take long, but when she arrived Doc Rene looked tired and grim. She was usually unflappable. As the only healing witch on the island, and the person who did the autopsies on the previous victims, she'd seen a lot.

"Magda Potter died from a broken neck, specifically a fracture of the second cervical vertebra," she said, pulling out her tablet to show us images I really didn't want to see but forced myself to look at, anyway. "The break is consistent with a violent twisting motion applied with significant force."

"Could it have been an accident?" I asked, even though I already knew the answer.

"No. The angle and force required couldn't happen from a fall or stumble. This was deliberate." Doc Rene swiped to another image. "But here's what's particularly concerning. I found traces of a suppression spell all over her clothes. It is designed to dampen her ability to read hostile intent. I don't know what other use it has, but I can look."

Mrs. V leaned forward. "Show me."

The two of them bent over the tablet and muttered. I hated not knowing what was going on, but I couldn't ask Tulip. She'd make me an offer I shouldn't accept.

"This is sophisticated work," Mrs. V said finally. "The spell need time to get to full strength. At least a day. Did she complain about her powers?"

"No," I said as I tried to remember our interactions. "A headache. And that started yesterday. She said someone wasn't who they pretended to be, but no details."

"That changes things," Mark said. "Magda didn't die because she accidentally discovered something. She died because someone decided she was a threat and spent over twenty-four hours preparing to kill her without her abilities warning her. The headache might have been a reaction to the spell."

"The killer must be one of my three remaining

students," I said. "They're the only ones who had access to Magda since she arrived. The others wandered a bit, but she stuck to The Inner Spell. I don't think anyone from the island visited."

D made a thinking grunt and looked up from the results of his searching. "Unless there's someone else with access your place we don't know about. Someone who could get in and out without being noticed."

"I would have seen or felt something," I said, but even as I spoke, uncertainty rose up. Had I been paying close enough attention? I'd been so focused on managing my own anxiety about teaching that I might have missed someone observing from outside the tent or using concealment magic to stay hidden. "You know anyone on the island can access the place unless it's locked up. I wanted The Inner Spell to feel accessible, no locks on anything but the private rooms."

I chose not to mention the people who had official access. Zinnia used to manage the retreat. Lance, D, Lilibeth, all had a hand in creating the place. Zoe, Sheena, and Jan supplied us with food. I couldn't believe people I trusted would do such an evil thing.

"The wards I placed don't care about authorized or not," Mrs. V said. "I'll recognize the signature of your regulars. But for now, we should operate on the assumption that our killer is Samuel Whitlock, Jasper Sturn, or Ravi Jain."

Mark flipped to a new page in his notebook. "Let's build profiles. What do we know about each of them, and what are the gaps in our knowledge?"

D pulled up files on his laptop. "Starting with Samuel Whitlock. Age thirty-four, originally from a community in Oregon. Family background checks out—parents were members of their council, both deceased as of three years ago. Samuel's education claims are harder to verify because his family tradition was private tutoring rather than formal schooling."

I'd never considered that the magical world was so like the plain one. I guess it made sense if you had the money you would want to control the way your kids were educated.

"His employment history shows work in magical community organizing and dispute resolution," D continued. "References are all positive but generic—the kind of thing you'd write for someone you worked with briefly but didn't know well. Social media presence is minimal and only goes back about six years. That's ours. I haven't started on the plain human platforms yet. He might have an account there."

"Why only six years?" I asked. "I would expect someone his age to be using social media from his early teens."

D shrugged. "Could be he purged old accounts. Could be he didn't use social media before then. He might be embarrassed by what he posted at first."

Mark made a note. "What about Jasper Sturn?"

"Jasper's easier to verify," D said. "He seems completely open about his life. Born in Washington, moved to Kamloops five years ago with his wife, Charlotte. She died recently. The council ruled it an accident. Something went wrong in a warding spell."

"Do you have the details?" I asked. "He's still in a lot of pain over the incident. If he isn't the killer, I'm not sure I can let him be a protector until he's dealt with his grief."

"I can request the full report." Mark made a note under the heading ACTION in his notebook.

I relayed what I'd learned about him. "He blames someone for Charlotte's death. He said his wife died because someone with proper training wasn't there to intervene. What if he's targeting people he sees as incompetent protectors?"

"Magda was a teacher, not a protector," D pointed out. "The only protectors on Henbane are you and Mrs. V. until you get them through the training."

"It's possible he's not thinking straight," Mrs. V said with more sympathy than I expected. "Grief can drive people to seek revenge for imagined slights. You'll need to go deeper to find the answer. I'm sure you're up to it, Cossi."

I hadn't expected the compliment. "What about Ravi? Did we get anyone right?"

D pulled up another file. "Ravi Jain, age twenty-six. Bachelor's degree in environmental science from UC Berkeley, master's in ecological magic from a small private university. His thesis was on Aggressive Intervention Strategies for Magical Ecosystem Restoration."

"Aggressive intervention," Mrs. V repeated. "That's concerning language."

"His academic adviser noted in his file that Ravi was passionate to the point of zealotry about environmental protection and recommended he develop more balanced perspectives before entering fieldwork," D said. "I guess it's hard to stay on the rational side when the planet is at stake."

"So all three of them have concerning elements," I said. "Samuel with the gaps in his background. Jasper with his grief-driven anger and possible revenge motive. Ravi with his environmental extremism."

"Which means we're back to square one," Mark said. "Three equally viable suspects, no clear evidence pointing to any of them specifically."

7

I'd hoped for something to isolate the potential killer. I guess we all had.

"You should punish everyone of your suspects. The truth will come out then," Destroyer announced. "Tulip agrees."

I wasn't going to annoy him by asking Tulip to confirm his statement. I didn't think any of the animals could lie, anyway. And really it wasn't a surprise that the lynx took the violent side.

"We need to create opportunities for evidence to emerge," Mrs. V said. "Continue the training program, but with each of us assigned specific roles in observation and protection."

That was a nicer way than Destroyer's of sorting out the killer.

"We will have to tell them she's gone. And I still need to grow the number of protectors. It's not like the murder put off the larger problem," I pointed out. "Unless you think all three were involved, we have two innocent candidates.

Maybe three because we have no real proof one of my students did it."

"Cossi is right," Mrs. V said. "We contain this now, while we have all three suspects in one place and a legitimate reason to keep them under observation. And the opportunity to produce at least two more protectors."

Mark looked like he wanted to argue about who's priority was more urgent, but D spoke up first. "Keep them confined to The Inner Spell. If you need them to meet other residents, invite people to join you. Like you did with Jeffery. Any of us can place wards to stop them wandering."

"And I'll attend sessions as a guest instructor," Mrs. V said. "We planned that as part of the curriculum, anyway. I will increase my presence beyond what we expected. And if someone tries to run, Tulip can track them."

I didn't relish the idea of having a feline thug around, but I couldn't think of a reason for her to stay at the cottage. And Mrs. V was the oldest protector. More of her training would be valuable. As much as she insisted we were peers, I still felt like she was the boss.

"I'll conduct formal interviews with all three students," Mark added. "Establish alibis, and use my powers to catch any obvious deceptions. The usual. It might lead us to more suspects."

"We'll do it together," I said. "My emotion reading might help clear up any ambiguity. I could let you know when to dig deeper, or back off."

"You teach," Mrs. V said. "And you observe. I will not allow you to be distracted from the most important need. Protectors."

She was worried I couldn't do both. I saw it in the mustard spikes in her emotions. No point in arguing with her because I'd do what was needed and deal with the repercussions.

"What about the other students?" I asked. "How do we protect the innocent ones while investigating the guilty one?"

"We don't tell them they're suspects," Mark said. "Not yet. We tell them Magda's death is under investigation. And they are potential witnesses. Maybe the killer will slip up and ask something that gives them away."

"Like a question only a murderer would ask," I said. "Good plan if we say it was an accident."

"Let them suspect," Mrs. V said. "Their reactions to the investigation might tell us something useful."

My phone rang—Jasper. I put it on speaker.

"Cossi, Mr. Peak told us the rest of the training today is postponed," he said, his voice tight with concern. "What's going on? Is everyone okay?"

"There's been an accident," I said, trying to keep my voice steady. "Magda was injured at the training facility. We're sorting out what happened."

There was a pause. "Injured how badly?"

I looked at Mark, who shook his head slightly. I wasn't exactly eager to add to his trauma.

"We're still assessing the situation," I said. "I'll have more information soon. In the meantime, I need you to stay available for questions from Mark Justin. He'll be conducting interviews with all the students to figure out how it happened."

"Of course," Jasper said. "Whatever you need. Is Magda going to be okay?"

The genuine concern in his voice could have been real or could have been an excellent performance. I had no way to tell. He still radiated pain. "I'll update you as soon as I can," I said, and ended the call.

"He didn't know she was dead," D said. "Or he's a very good actor."

"I'll note the time of the call and his exact words," Mark said, writing in his notebook. "We'll compare reactions from all three students."

Our tasks were set. Mark would interview the students as soon as D had the deeper background checks completed. I would keep the three remaining students—I refused to continue to think of them as suspects—occupied and unaware of the murder details. Mrs. V would join us in the morning to start her master classes.

"One more thing," she said as we were wrapping up. "A witch with Magda's empathic abilities usually keeps a journal of her observations and feelings about people. If she sensed something wrong about one of the students, she might have documented it."

"I'll check her room," Mark said. "If there's a journal, it might tell us who she suspected."

"Be careful," I said. "If the killer thinks Magda left evidence, they might try to retrieve it."

"Good," Mark said grimly. "Let them try. I'll be waiting."

As the meeting broke up and everyone headed to their assigned tasks, D pulled me aside.

"Are you sure about this?" he asked. "Being alone with suspects is a big risk. I mean you sleep up there. Maybe Lance or I should move in."

"I think that might make them suspicious," I said. "I can make a new exclusion ward for my suite. Like the one Mark gave me before." The little red bag in my room in Phillip's apartment wouldn't let anyone but me enter.

D wanted to argue. I saw it in his aura and his face, but

instead he just pulled me into a brief, tight hug. "Be careful. Please."

He was so sweet. I still wasn't ready to choose between him or Mark as my... ugh boyfriend was so juvenile. "I will. You too. The killer will know you're investigating soon enough."

I sat alone in Mrs. V's kitchen with a cup of tea I didn't want and tried to process everything that had happened in the last six hours.

"A wise emperor adapts to changing battlefield conditions," Destroyer observed.

"This isn't a battlefield," I said. I wouldn't let it get that far. This was my home and every tree, shrub, and rock was precious.

"We think it's adorable that you pretend you have a choice. Do not remain so gullible."

He wasn't wrong. Later I would stand in front of Samuel, Jasper, and Ravi and teach them about protector ethics and abilities while knowing one of them was a murderer. I would smile and encourage questions and facilitate discussions, all while watching for signs of guilt or dangerous intent.

It was going to be the hardest thing I'd ever done.

8

I hadn't slept. Every time I closed my eyes, I saw Magda's body on the meditation tent floor, positioned as if she'd simply laid down to rest. By five AM, I gave up trying and went to the training facility to prepare for what would be the strangest teaching day of my life.

D had installed cameras overnight—small, discreet and masked so they wouldn't be detected. This was one of those times when mundane tech was more useful than magic because the power to record and play back was specialized. No one on Henbane could do it and to be honest, I suspected that D's tech magic helped more than his training.

"I'll be watching everything in real time," he said, showing me the feeds on his laptop. "Any sign of trouble, I'm ten seconds away from helping you."

"Thank you," I said, meaning it more than I expected. If trouble came, I figured my protector power would take over, but knowing he was there as backup was comforting.

Mrs. V arrived next, carrying a collection of protective amulets. "Wear this," she said, handing me a simple silver bracelet. "It won't stop a direct attack, but it'll give you instant shielding if someone tries to harm you. It will give D and Mark enough time to get to you."

I suddenly felt like the peaceful retreat I'd created was under attack. Yes, there'd been a murder. It wasn't the first time a body showed up here. We'd cleansed after Mrs. Macy's case was solved so it wasn't a case of the site being tainted. I pushed the thought back. This was a separate incident and Mrs. Macy wasn't killed here. "Are you going to watch too? We can say you're observing my methods."

"I'm here as a guest instructor," she said. "Someone who has more experience. You've been more of a detective than protector until now. Is something wrong? We discussed this yesterday. I thought you were paying attention."

The memory hit as she asked. "I guess there's a lot for me to remember."

She gave me a hard stare but didn't say anything. I tried not to think she was disappointed in me.

By the time Mark arrived with Roy, we were almost ready to go.

"Where should I set up?" Mark asked. "I'll get the interviews done as quickly as I can. It's only preliminary, so you should be able to go on teaching like we planned."

I showed him the corner we'd set up. In the range of two cameras so D would have the recording, and Mark could concentrate on reactions.

Roy twitched his ears. "Wrong."

I looked at him to let Mark know we were talking. "What's wrong exactly?"

"Don't know."

I told Mark and Mrs. V what he'd said. "If Roy says something's wrong, we should stay alert. I mean more alert, I guess."

"Roy, you can patrol until you find the problem," Mark said.

"I'll let you know if he finds anything," I told him. If I couldn't manage to train students, maybe I'd find a job as an animal to human translator.

"Dolph told me he'd set a few shifters to guard," Mark said as he set up. "They'll camp in the trees. Ready to track, or capture. I'll ask them to check for weirdness when I go."

D came over to adjust the cameras. "That was a good idea. If our suspect runs, a shifter is the best tracker."

Mrs. V smiled, something I'd barely gotten used to. "Better than that, they can keep an eye on where our suspects wander during their free time. We won't need to create a secure area. If they think they are free, we our killer might make a mistake.."

Samuel as usual arrived first. He looked tired but composed, dressed in the same casual style that projected the image of a serious student. Teacher's pet energy was oozing from him.

"I came early in case you needed help setting up," he said. "I know yesterday was... I can't imagine how difficult this must be for you. For all of us." His concern seemed genuine, his offer of help sincere.

"Thank you," I said. "Mark needs to speak with you about yesterday." I pointed him to where Mark was standing beside the table holding his notebook and phone.

From my position, I couldn't hear the interview, we'd purposefully set it up that way. I joined D at his laptop. Samuel sat and answered questions pausing to think before speaking. He maintained steady eye contact with Mark. I don't know what I expected, but Samuel didn't strike me as having something to hide. It was over before either of the other two students wandered in.

Jasper joined us followed by Ravi. Jasper looked like he hadn't slept—or his sleep was filled with nightmares. The grief-driven anger I'd noticed before had grown to drown his other emotions to pale shadows.

"Is she really dead?" he asked abruptly, not bothering with pleasantries. "I can't believe it's happened here. Henbane is supposed to be a haven."

"Hey, don't blame Cossi," Ravi said.

"Mark is investigating Magda's death," I said as gently as I could. "He'll talk to each of you now that Samuel is finished."

Jasper's face contorted with rage—his emotions boiling around him in a violent rainbow. "Another death. Another person who died because—" He stopped himself, breathing hard. "I won't wait until he calls me. I need to get this done."

He stalked toward the interview table before I could stop him.

He passed Samuel, throwing a glare his way and sat across from Mark. I heard Ravi mutter something about looking guilty but ignored it.

The interview with Jasper took longer and seemed more contentious. I moved away from D because I didn't want to give away that he was recording. Having done that, I had no idea how to fill the time. I didn't plan to start teaching until all three interviews were complete.

Rave stood facing the interview. His emotions a dark swirl. Not of guilt or fear. He was sad and worried. It didn't mean he was innocent. "Actions like this can damage the ecology. I know it sounds kind of out there, but the health of the land is tied to the people as well as the water and nutrients."

"Mark's going to figure out what happened," I said. "It

could be an accident. Those happen all the time. We'll continue with our lessons until he has the answers."

"How many possibilities are there? If it wasn't an accident then Magda was murdered." Ravi's expression shifted from distress to cold logic. His emotions drew in close to his body. "Was it someone from outside the program? One of the residents brought a stranger in? Someone who doesn't want protector training to succeed?"

The speed with which he jumped to external threats was interesting. Either he genuinely hadn't considered that a student might be responsible, or he was very good at deflecting suspicion.

Pretending murder wasn't an option would just make everything worse. I needed these three witches to believe me. Until we had more information, the truth was it could have been an accident.

"It's probably not murder. And if it is, those aren't the only options. People come here for festivals. Anyone of them could have made their way back." I didn't believe a stranger arriving would have been kept secret for long. If the council didn't have ward to alert them, then Destroyer's network of land and air spies would have told me.

"I didn't think of that," Ravi said. "I guess we're all used to thinking of Henbane as a secure place. Where witches are safe even from normal things."

"Mark will ask you about what you observed yesterday," I said. "He will need all the facts before he can determine the manner of death. Doc Rene is doing the tests. I'm sure we'll have answers soon."

It took Mark only about ten minutes to make note of everything Ravi told him. I let the others pour their tea and take a few cookies while we waited. I noticed Ravi checking his field journal and making more notes as Mark waited. I suppose his interest and powers in the ecology of the island took him on longer walks than the others. He might have seen something helpful.

Mark joined me when he was done and escorted me outside as if that would mean we had some privacy. "Not much to go on," he said. "D will stay. He told your students his job is to gather data to improve the curriculum."

"Do you have any impressions?" I asked. "Was anyone lying? Does one of them have a shifty alibi?"

"Everyone lies about something," he said. "Samuel is either completely innocent or an exceptional liar. My power didn't catch anything important, but he's very controlled."

Everything about Samuel was controlled. I didn't have any experience with wealthy people witches or plain humans—but from watching period dramas, I imagine stiff upper lip is lesson one. "What about Jasper? He seemed a little calmer when you finished with him."

"He's emotionally volatile but honest about it. I guess it's good that he recognizes he hasn't dealt well with his grief, but I told him to talk to Doc Rene. The man needs to process or... I guess I don't know. I got the sense his lies are about grief. I can't see him killing, but you never know."

I'd talk to her too. We had her findings. Her part of the investigation was done and she'd have time to do some healing—I'd put money on her preferring that. "And Ravi? He's pretty passionate."

Mark started to roll his eyes but stopped himself. "Cooperative to the point of being almost too eager to help. The guy is observant; I guess that comes with his power and research. He had theories." He glanced at the entrance to make sure we still had privacy, before continuing. "He talks so much that I can't help thinking he was evading my questions. Every answer he gave was thorough but also managed to paint himself in the best possible light. Savior of the planet and all that. I found it hard to keep pressing."

So all three of them had passed Mark's initial screening without any obvious red flags, but all three had concerning elements in their presentations. We were exactly where we'd started—with three viable suspects and no clear evidence. And a faint suspicion that my students were innocent. It felt like we kept going in the same circles and I had to remind myself it was only day one. This case felt heavy on my heart, but maybe that was just me.

"Mrs. V found something in Magda's room," Mark added, handing me a small notebook. "Her journal. She kept notes on everyone she interacted with, including the students."

I opened the journal to the pages marked with the faint glow of Mrs. V's magic. Magda's handwriting was spiky but easily read. She worked in a field that required legibility because of things like peer review. Or at least transcribing notes in to an app.

I read the entries since she'd arrived.

Day one of Protector training. We spent much time on introductions. Samuel Whitlock: Very polished presentation. Helpful, engaged, asks good questions. But something feels performed? Like he's following a script for ideal student behavior. I believe his polish is hiding something he needs to heal.

Jasper Sturn: Carrying enormous grief. Anger directed at systems/authority more than individuals. Frequently mentions wife died due to incompetence. I suggested he talk to the local doctor to ease his pain. He didn't feel this damaged on the way over.

Ravi Jain: Enthusiastic and idealistic on surface. Deeper read shows intense conviction that borders on zealotry. Believes strongly that current practices are inadequate for environmental protection. That our job as magical humans is to repair what is done.

Day 2. Something is definitely wrong. During meditation exercise, felt multiple conflicting emotions in the room. Someone is working very hard to project appropriate responses while hiding true emotional state. Can't pinpoint who—the concealment is multi-layered. On a personal note, the headache is getting worse. Possibly because I am so disturbed by this dissonance.

"She knew something was wrong, and thought it could be any of them," I said, rereading the notes. "But she couldn't pinpoint which one was the real threat. No notes on me, though. There should be, I'm just as much a stranger as the other students."

"You are a protector. Everyone trusts you because of that," Mark said. "But her notes confirm that someone was using magic to hide who they are during the sessions."

Mrs. V poked her head out. She'd been setting up her guest instructor materials in different areas of the tent. "The students are getting restless. We should start the session before they start comparing notes about the interviews."

I took a deep breath, tucked Magda's journal into my bag, and prepared to teach a class that included her murderer.

9

The three students sat in the discussion tent, arranged in a triangle that meant no one had their back completely to anyone else. Maybe I was the only one to notice that fact. Samuel looked composed and attentive. Jasper looked angry and exhausted. Ravi looked shaken but determined. So nothing new.

"Good morning," I said, hoping they bought the calm authority I was going for but didn't feel. "We are going to proceed with our lesson. Not as if nothing happened, that would be impossible especially for protectors. D is going to be with us. He'll keep notes to help me refine the training."

"Mrs. V is also observing, right?" Jasper asked, nodding toward where she was sitting near the back of the tent. "It's an honor to have her here."

"Mrs. Vestum has knowledge of the history we need," I said. "Other protectors will be offered the chance to teach in future courses." If there was a future. We were down one candidate already and the learning hadn't started.

"Are we suspects?" Ravi asked bluntly. "No, I suppose

that's not the right question. We must be suspects. But are there others?"

The directness caught me off guard, but I decided honesty was the best approach. "Everyone who had access to the facility yesterday is being interviewed to establish what happened. That's standard procedure. Mark will follow every lead to find the killer if he determines her death was not an accident."

Samuel shifted uncomfortably. "But we're protector candidates. We were vetted. Magda's death must have been an accident or caused by someone outside the program."

The tension in the room spiked. Mrs. V moved slightly, positioning herself where she could intervene quickly if needed. Her hand was in her pocket, sorting through charms. I hated that I didn't know if she was seeking a calming, or a restraint spell.

"What we know," I said carefully, "is that Magda died in a way that couldn't have been an accident. Until we understand what happened, we need to be careful and watchful. That means additional supervision, enhanced security, and yes, investigation of everyone who was present."

"Including you?" Ravi asked. "Or is this just us? The incomers."

"Including me," I confirmed. "Mark interviewed me for over an hour last night."

I was glad no one in the tent had lie detection powers. Interviewed was a bit of a gray area. The subject wasn't my innocence, but my knowledge of the three students in this tent.

My words seemed to ease some of the tension. The reactions were natural because each one was different. If Mrs. V used magic, the effect would have been the same. Samuel continued to cover his emotions behind his shield, but he nodded acceptance. Jasper didn't argue back but I think he was too deep in his own pain to care. Ravi just seemed open to any information.

"Today we'll start with exploring the extent of a protector's duties," I said. "Magda knew the danger of not having enough protectors. She wouldn't want us to delay developing more."

"Agreed," Samuel said immediately. "Though I think we should acknowledge that this will be difficult for all of us. We've lost a colleague, and we're understandably shaken. It may take more time to think through the complexities."

"What's that supposed to mean?" Ravi asked. "Are you implying we can't focus?"

"It means you're taking notes like this is a research project instead of a person dying," Jasper said. "It means Samuel's acting like this is a professional setback instead of a tragedy. It means nobody seems actually upset."

If Jasper couldn't get past the rawness of his wife's death, he might need to defer his place here. I couldn't let him keep derailing the progress.

"People process grief differently," Mrs. V said, saving me from having to deal with the situation. Her tone sharp enough to cut through the rising tension which might be the reason their attention fixed on her. "And judging each other's emotional responses isn't productive. And it will not show us you have the potential to protect our world. If you want to continue this program, you need to work together. If you can't get control of yourself, the door is right there."

I needed to develop that grumpy no-nonsense tone. And fast. Mrs. V might have been born with it, but I couldn't rely on her to be around to fill the role of taskmaster.

Nobody moved. After a moment, Jasper looked away, his jaw clenched. Samuel made a small apologetic gesture and

Ravi closed his journal. He didn't put it away, and I hoped he knew I would let him take all the notes he needed.

Perhaps the issue, beyond Magda's death, was these people were all fully formed with their own experiences and biases. The only alternative I could think up was to train younger candidates. We didn't really have time for that though, and testing a program on kids seemed like an ethical violation. Maybe when we had a few more protectors on the ground, we could start with teens, maybe younger.

"Let's focus on training," I said. "Today we're going to work on recognition exercises—learning to identify the difference between strong personal convictions and actual protector authority. Mrs. V will demonstrate some advanced techniques."

The session proceeded without other conflict. Mrs. V showed them how protector abilities manifested differently from ordinary strong opinions. Samuel asked intelligent questions and participated thoughtfully. I wished they all did the same, but Ravi was back with his extensive note taking as if he just needed to absorb to understand.

Jasper remained quiet but attentive, though I noticed him watching the other two students more than he watched the demonstration. He was the one I worried about most. Yes, because of his pain, but also I had no hint if he was learning.

During a break, while the students were getting coffee, Mrs. V pulled me aside.

"They're all performing," she said quietly. "Samuel's acting the role of competent student. Ravi's showing us how much of a dedicated researcher he is. Jasper's hiding behind his grieving widower and trying not to show us how hurt he is. I can't determine yet which performance is covering murder if any of them are."

Every clue that led toward proving one of my students being a killer was like a cut into my heart. We missed some aspect in the screening. Even without Magda's death, these candidates couldn't be the best.

This kind of situation was where I missed growing up as a witch the most. I was relying on my false expectation that witches were better than plain humans. "Can you tell anything from their actions during the exercises? Is there something we need to do for them to show their true intentions?"

"All three have more training than they admitted in their applications," she said. "Samuel's control is exceptional—too good for someone with the education and background he gave. The other two maybe not so much but just as concerning. Jasper's a metal witch, that comes with a lot of strength he can use against someone. I'm not sure if Ravi fully accepts his own magic, or the potential. Something is holding him back."

"How could all three of them lie about their capabilities? And if these three did, what was Magda hiding?"

There was that look again, like I was stating the obvious. Okay, I was, but it still felt like a rebuke.

"Her death could be a consequence of hiding something, but you need to stop asking and start making your own conclusions."

So not just feels like a rebuke. I agreed with her, but it was too easy to ask when she was standing right beside me.

D sent me a text. *It might be nothing, but Samuel checked his phone during the break and his expression changed. Only a flash, but definitely relief. I might be able to get his messages.*

Another text followed before I could reply: *Why would Ravi use code in his notebook?*

Every observation made me feel like I was betraying

their trust. I knew we had no choice, but this was so intrusive. I sent a reply: *No hacking phones without Mark's permission. No taking pictures of notebooks. Keep an eye on Jasper unless you have something else to say right now.*

He sent back a smiley emoji but no other details.

The afternoon session was more practical—having the students try to identify situations where protector authority would be appropriate versus situations where it would be overreach. Kind of role playing. Mrs. V and I gave feedback, and I almost forgot that D was watching everything to find a killer.

All the students brought value to the exercise. Samuel excelled at theoretical analysis. Ravi brought a more strategic viewpoint which made sense with his environmental powers. Hard to think about mundane details when you usually focused on saving the planet. Jasper contributed less but seemed to be absorbing everything. I regained a shred of confidence we'd chosen wisely and the killer wasn't in this group.

As the day ended and the students prepared to leave, Samuel approached me with his usual offer of help. I tried to take it as kindness, but a big part of me wanted to ask him if he thought I couldn't handle the job.

"I know this is a difficult time," he said. "If there's anything I can do to support the program, please let me know. I have experience with crisis management."

It was a generous offer. Unfortunately, I thought it was also exactly what a killer might say to stay close to the investigation.

"Thank you," I said. "I'll keep that in mind. But remember you are here to learn not solve my problems."

After everyone left, the investigation team reconvened in the practical tent. It was time to share and dissect everything we'd learned. Or to be more precise, everything we'd gathered—I had no idea if we'd learned anything.

"Any news from your animals?" Mark asked. "They've been really useful before."

"No one has come forward," I said. "I'm kind of hard to reach inside the building. I'll sleep in one of the chalets tonight. Or, I can go out to them. Maybe have a chat with Lance."

"I have no information," Destroyer announced. "Therefore no information exists. None of my subjects would keep secrets from their benevolent emperor."

I passed that along. "I'll still leave the opportunity open. I'm not sure the animals Destroyer thinks of as his subjects agree."

"That is impossible." He sent me an image of what would happen to a disloyal subject. It involved eagles and dinner.

"Do not allow that to happen." I didn't often order him around, but he was my familiar and wouldn't be able to go against my direct order. It didn't work the other way around thank whoever runs the universe. "Also, I don't need the visuals."

"Magda's notes said someone was using a strong shield to hide behind," I said, turning my attention back to the investigation. "Can we identify who based on today's observations?"

"All three showed signs of emotional control," Mrs. V said. "But that's not uncommon for people under stress in a high-stakes situation and I saw nothing that said the control was coming from an external source. The killer's concealment during the actual murder would have been more extensive. And what we all saw could be related to the opportunity to become a protector."

"So we're still at square one," D said.

"Not quite," Mark said. "We know how she died. We know everyone on our suspect list has secrets. We do need a plan to dig deeper. I'm not sure invading privacy is our next step, but it's on the list." Mark didn't need authorization to hack into messages, or demand a notebook for analysis. He preferred to hold back on those tactics until he had more evidence.

"It's not a lot," I said. "I really need to talk to whoever stole the pastries. Not a mouse, too small, but maybe a squirrel. Yeah, like I said I should head into the trees later and ask again."

"Let's the shifters know," Mark said. "They can keep you safe."

From what? I'd never felt threatened by any of the animals on Henbane. "And they'll scare away whoever I need to question." I held up my hand before he could object. "I'll tell them to stay far enough away."

10

Usually when I enter the forest, there's all kinds of chatter. This time the shifters must be scaring my sources away. I couldn't hear even the light buzz of insects. I didn't understand that language. Maybe it wasn't one, or maybe I needed to spend time focusing on my own powers.

Lance called my name before stepping from behind an oak tree. "Any news?"

I shook my head. "I'm going to talk to whoever's around. Someone tried to steal some leftovers, so I'm hopeful they saw something."

"There's a shield," he said tilting his head in the direction of The Inner Spell.

"Mrs. V set up wards," I said. "Just alarms, though. It shouldn't chase anyone away."

He looked around us like he was expecting a lurker. "Not hers. This happened yesterday. Anyone who was at the location when the shield went up can come and go, but everyone else fights a faint sense of dread when they come close."

And the animals would sense that. No wonder I hadn't seen any all day. "Is it bothering your team? Should I talk to Dolph?" I didn't want to get tangled in shifter politics, but if Lance needed help, I'd give it a try.

"We got a charm from Valerie to damp it down," he said. "The dread is still there but we can handle it. We're not trying to get in anyway. I can text if I need you. I do have an update if you have time."

Of course I wanted information. Was the shield affecting his ability to tell me anything that would lead to the killer? "Yes. I have no idea what the three students do when I'm not teaching them. We decided to put our energy into solving the crime rather than monitoring."

"Only two wander," he said. "I've had them followed. Ravi goes around at all hours making notes, taking samples. We can't get close, but I think he's trying to figure out if there's a difference on Henbane. Like we have a secret we won't share that will stop climate change."

Not a big surprise. "I'm worried about him. He's so focused on the ecology. I can't let him be a protector if he only looks at one thing."

"I don't envy you the job," Lance said. "The other guy is a bit creepy. He goes out on the road checking for signal. At least that's what we thought because it can be spotty out here. Then when he gets enough bars, he calls someone. Because he's out in the open we can't get close enough, even with our hearing, to catch everything. We got enough to guess he's reporting to someone. Not what he's telling them."

Probably his family, I thought. "Why do you think he's creepy?"

"We can't read people like you do," Lance said. He leaned against the tree and closed his eyes like he needed to get rid of all distractions. "People give off a vibe—I hate the word, but it's the only one that fits. Mostly people are a mix of good and shady. Not many people are bad. None here at least. But we missed Phillip, so it's not infallible. Samuel doesn't have one."

"A vibe?" How was that possible? Just being alive meant he had experiences. "Did Elias have a vibe? Is it about emotions?" Phillip had stolen Elias's emotions to support his illusion of normalcy.

"It's about everything. Elias did have a vibe. It's stronger now." He looked around again shrugging as if he had an itch. "That shield is getting to me."

"Do you know where the closest squirrel is hanging out?" I would let him go because he was too close to the magic. Mrs. V would find a way to remove the shield, and maybe figure out who placed it there.

"You need to go about a hundred meters." Lance pointed deeper into the trees. "I'll send a text if I learn something important. Or if the shield changes"

I watched him slide into the shadows before setting off into the forest. I called out to Destroyer, but he told me he was too busy with Imperial priorities. I never knew what he meant when he put me off that way. It could be searching for clues, convincing another flock or herd to join the Empire, or just flying around surveying his realm.

When I got close to the location Lance indicated, something seemed to slip from my body. I hadn't noticed the effect of the shield until it was gone. That was pretty subtle work. I wished it made a difference, but any of the students could have cast something like that.

I wasn't dealing with kids. These people had more decades of experience being witches than I did. Being a protector didn't erase my first twenty-one years of passing as a plain human. Although, that wasn't even accurate. You weren't passing as anything if you didn't know who you were.

I noticed a twitch of movement ahead of me. Halfway up the trunk of a huge redwood, a squirrel was twitching in excitement. Her eyes were firmly locked onto mine.

"Will you talk?" I asked. "Have you heard about me?"

"You are the protector who feeds," she said scurrying down to my height. "I am Squall Runner."

I'd spent most of my first months forgetting to ask for names. I appreciated her telling me up-front. Squirrels had a wide range of name styles. From Bob to Extreme Hunter of Acorns. "Do you know about the happenings?"

"Dead witch, again," she said cocking her head to the side. "Saw body. Took good tasting food. Dropped one when someone came."

She'd been waiting for me to come. I'd gotten much better at reading the emotions of animals in my time on Henbane. "Did you see anyone with the body?"

"Need to pay, not seeds. Need more good tasting food."

Pastries. Were they okay for squirrels to eat. I didn't want to be responsible for an outbreak of obesity. "Do you know information?"

"Yes. Can't come to your nest. Feels bad to get close. Not before but now."

The shield. "Tell me what you know, and I'll bring pastries to you. Five pastries." I'd make sure they were healthier than cream puffs.

"Deal. One of your new males came from the tent. I thought it was empty, so I went in to harvest. Female already smelled dead." She skittered up the trunk and then returned. It was hard for her to stand still long enough for a meaningful conversation. "Bring pastries when sun goes down. To here."

"Can you tell me what the male witch looked like?" Her ability to describe would be limited, but my students didn't look similar. I might get lucky.

"Shimmery. Sometimes yellow hair like straw, sometimes black like night. Covered up. Smelled like male, but maybe a female wearing male clothes."

"Taller than me?"

"All witches tall to us," she said. "I want payment tonight."

I promised to bring or send someone with the payment. Squall Runner chittered a warning about failure and ran up the tree.

I sent a text to D and Lance about delivering the food, so I didn't need to split my focus from the clues. I put out a call to the local birds and ground animals, but no one answered.

WHEN I GOT BACK, I updated everyone about the shield and the witness. Mrs. V left to test the components of the magic, annoyed she hadn't noticed it. D filled a small basket with leftovers and smiled. Squall Runner was getting far more than I'd promised.

"Everyone here is capable of casting a glamor," Mark said. "Too bad we don't have more witness reports."

"It's looking more and more like our killer is right here at The Inner Spell," I said. "We need more details about everyone. Even Magda. Maybe there's something in her history that will explain why she was killed now and not any other time."

"I'll go deeper," D said. "Finish the afternoon session

without me. I'll go home. I can drop off the payment to Lance so he can pass it on. I'll let Mrs. V know what happens as I leave the shield limits. I have a few not so ethical apps on my home system that might get me in to more relevant databases."

My protector power twitched when he admitted that. "You can't violate privacy unless it means protecting the world."

"Yeah, I know." He tucked his laptop in his backpack. "I can't get you information without breaking the rules, but we keep it between us. Even if we're right and you have a killer here. You have two innocents, and the victim."

He left and I sent a group text for the students to join me for the afternoon sessions. We were still in the sorting out phase. I couldn't plan real training until I knew more about the individuals. When we started, we'd decided to keep the classes small so I could tailor the training to each candidate. Our goal was to fill some gaps, not push out waves and waves of protectors.

11

D called me to join him for dinner. He'd found something we needed to see in person and going to his place meant we wouldn't be overheard.

As I passed out of the shield, I felt that lift of weight again. It wasn't just a psychic thing. Suddenly I heard birds, and Destroyer muttering to himself. How had I not noticed the missing sound of life? I mean, yes, I noticed it when I left, but inside? The more I learned the less I like the idea of a witch who could layer so many spells being a killer.

"Before we get into the checks," D said as he dished out burgers and fries from Jan's place. "What's happening with the shield?"

I remember a day when no one dared to ask Mrs. V questions like that. No wonder she was more friendly—okay not that, but at least less grumpy—these days.

"I've looked through the layers," she said. "It acts as an alarm for whoever placed it, much like mine does for us. It's also thickening the air. If we don't remove it you will suffer from hypoxia in a few days. It also has a component for enhancing illusions. I can remove it when you're ready."

"Not yet," Mark said. "I don't want the killer to be alarmed. Too dangerous."

"Do you think the spell could have gone wrong?" I asked. "Like someone tossed up a protection to keep a killer from attacking, and the rest is an accidental byproduct?"

She looked at me and then I heard Tulip purr-growling behind me. The lynx was draped across the tiles in D's kitchen. She flicked out her tongue to clean her face as she said, "Only you are so careless."

"I'm still hoping it's not one of the students," I said. "If we can't trust our screening, how are we going to train protectors?"

"You put too much on our first trial," Mrs. V said. "This is a step toward perfecting the process, yes? We hope to find a spell or power that will screen quickly."

I picked up a fry to avoid answering. She was right—always. I'd expected to send four protectors out to the world, and now it looked like none of these witches were going to make it.

"Let's go over what you found," Mark said. "We're not going to solve this with a deep dive into someone's private life unless one of them had killed before and bragged about it. My main hope is we achieve a pointer or two."

"Let's start with Samuel Whitlock," D said, highlighting sections of his report. "His story checks out on the surface— parents registered with Oregon magical council, family tradition of community service. But when you dig deeper, things get weird."

"Weird how?" I asked.

"His social media presence only goes back six years, which we already knew. But I managed to access some archived data from his college years." D pulled up screen-shots. "The Samuel Whitlock who attended those schools looks similar but not identical. Different bone structure in the face, different build. Could be weight loss and aging, or an illusion of aging, but..."

"You think it's a different person," Mark said. "Any way to prove it?"

"Like DNA? I don't have a sample from the school, so no. I'll give it more thought. I'm more concerned about his sense of boundaries. I got into his university records. His adviser made note of a disturbing pattern of behavior. Willingness to go a bit too far. It was only one year, and no other comments, but I looked at the history of the university. In that year there was a scandal about some secret society and criminal training."

Mrs. V glanced at Tulip, like the lynx was an expert in criminal behavior. "What kind of criminal training?"

"Memory manipulation, emotional projection, identity concealment," D said. "The kind of techniques used by people who need to blend into communities and avoid detection."

Not great. "Like to infiltrate?" I hadn't consciously thought of it, but I guess I'd hoped to leave conspiracy theories behind me.

"Exactly. Like he was training as a spy, or deep cover cop, or criminal. Hard to say which side he was on. And if you look at his records through that lens, it explains the lack of history. Someone scrubbed him."

That story he told about finding an illusion spell. This could all stem from his actions as a ten-year-old.

"So Samuel could be working under a false identity, but it could be on the right side of things or the wrong," Mark said. "It makes him a strong suspect for our murder. Or an ally in solving it."

"Except," I said, not wanting to narrow our focus on so

little evidence, "it could also mean he's running from something in his past. Maybe he has criminal training because he was forced into it and escaped. The identity change could be self-protection."

"Possible," Mrs. V said. "Also possible you watch too many crime shows. What about Jasper Sturn?"

D pulled up a different file. "Jasper's background is more verifiable but equally concerning. I got the full report on his wife Charlotte's death. The investigator ruled it accidental, but the circumstances are suspicious."

He displayed images of the accident report. "Charlotte Sturn died during a protection ritual that went wrong. She was part of a group trying to reinforce ward boundaries around a small community near Wallace Falls Park. The spell backfired, and the power feedback killed her instantly."

"Wards don't kill," Mrs. V said. "That sounds more like a hex or a recoil from something she cast."

"Something bad," I said. "Jasper might not know his wife as well as he thinks."

"I will send an envoy to the area," Destroyer announced. "It is time to expand my realm."

I told the others what my familiar was planning.

"Good idea," Mrs. V said. "Animals don't always remember but if the event was big enough, a bird might have noticed a clue."

I told Destroyer to let me know what he learned. There was no point in giving him permission, he would do what he wanted.

"The report is a bit thin on details," D said. "It's like the investigator decided it was an accident and stopped looking. No wonder Jasper is furious."

"I'll reach out," Mark said. "I recognize the name. We

met at a conference. I thought he was solid, but things change."

It surprised me every time I heard about witches doing normal things. Why wouldn't witch cops get together just like plain ones?

"Anything that will help us right away?" I asked because it felt like everything led to the fact we needed to be patient. I'd put money on the fact our students wouldn't be happy sticking around if it looked like the training was delayed or canceled. And when the shield dropped, who knew what would happen.

"I don't want to jump around," D said. "I have no idea what's useful or not. That's for you three to decide." He opened another file on his laptop.

Mark held up a hand to stop D from moving on. He was making notes. I'd once asked him why when everything would go on-line. He told me he liked to keep his own ideas at hand. I figured he knew better than me because I just relied on my memory.

"So Jasper has a possible motive if he blames the system for letting her death go unsolved," he said. "Why kill Magda? Did she have some connection to the ceremony, or the investigator?"

"And how did he pass the screening?" Mrs. V asked. "We were thorough so how did an angry witch get through?"

"I'll look into it," I said. "Doc Rene said he was just grieving. Maybe this level of anger is new." We would need to tighten the qualifications no matter how Jasper ended up here.

"I have more," D said. "Jasper's been researching combat. I did some digging and found out it's common for people with his experience to try to gain some control by getting stronger. But it would help him commit murder too."

"So he was trying to avoid being vulnerable?" I could understand the urge, but surely getting a handle on the anger was more important.

"We'll find out when I interview him again," Mark said. "Now we have details I can get closer to the truth."

"He's been ordering some questionable supplies," D added.

The list he opened on his screen was troubling, but not conclusive. All of them were traditional training weapons. Katanas, epees, the throwing stars were the most worrying. I tried not to ignore the warning signs, but I couldn't see someone who was so broken by a death twisting that into killing. At least not in the way Magda died. It would have been so much more violent and messy.

"When did he buy these?" I asked, hoping for a clear clue to his guilt or innocence.

"Starting three weeks ago. Right after he submitted his application for protector training."

The timing was damning. Jasper had applied for the program and immediately started acquiring materials that could be used to kill someone. Our screening wasn't just weak, it was useless.

"Maybe," I said, "he bought them because he genuinely wants to learn how to protect people and thought advanced tools would help with training."

"That's the problem with all of this," Mark said. "Every piece of evidence has an innocent explanation alongside the damning one. Not just for Jasper, all of them."

"What about Ravi?" I asked, almost dreading the answer.

D closed the list and opened a note file. "Ravi Jain is exactly who he claims to be. Environmental science background, educated in ecology from UBC. Looks like he formed the magical side of it through research. We don't have a discipline so it makes sense."

"We do have witches who are interested," Mrs. V said. "If he's not our killer, he might start building a whole school of thought."

"I've seen how passionate he is about environmental protection." I glanced down the list. "Passion isn't always facet of good balance."

D pulled up Ravi's academic records and highlighted sections of his thesis. "That might be the case here. His research focused on aggressive intervention strategies. To intervene in the activities of the plain world and prevent further damage through magic."

"That would threaten our whole world," Mrs. V said concern breaking through her shields. "Regardless of the murder, Cossi and I need to get to the bottom of his intentions. If he can't take the vows, I don't care how qualified he is."

"It gets worse," D said. "His academic adviser noted that Ravi proposed forming teams to address the worst offenders. He didn't mention magic, but we can read into his meaning. The adviser rejected the approach and advised him to focus on less high-risk plans."

"We don't know if he followed the advice, or just went underground," Mark said. "Has he talked about drastic measures?"

"He's definitely focused," I said. "I thought it was about learning how we managed and taking some methods to the mainland."

"Well, more information doesn't mean progress," Mark said. "That said, we have learned something. I can be more direct with my questions now. The thing that's missing is

Magda's background. We can't rely on D hacking, but I'm not sure how we do it otherwise."

This was so much more frustrating than the last few murders I'd helped to solve. Sometimes being on a hidden Island was isolating in a bad way. "D needs to search for information on Magda. Between us, Mark and I can pull the truth out of my students. It's hard to say, but being a murder victim doesn't make you a saint."

12

I t was late when Mark followed me to the tents. We checked in with Lance before passing through the shield.

"The animals are still keeping away," Lance said. "I don't like the feeling. It's weird because I don't usually notice them, but now it all feels like one of those zombie shows."

I knew what he meant and felt bad that I was going back to a nice bed in the main part of the retreat. "Mrs. V is working on it," I said. "Are any of my students wandering?"

"They were all taking walks," Lance said. "Ravi is the only one who seems to have a purpose other than getting some exercise. He keeps going to the river and taking samples. Seems a bit disappointed when he doesn't find anything bad."

I would be shocked if he did find a problem. I wouldn't drink from the river, because animals used it for more than drinking, but it was clean.

"We're going to start interrogations," Mark said. "I'm planning to push harder. We can't keep dithering. If the killer is here, Cossi and I will find them. If not, we need to know right away."

"Yeah. I'm guessing the shield is low on the list right now," Lance said, nodding his chin to the tents. "Roy doesn't like it, I see."

"He's been complaining of an itch since we got close," I said. "It wasn't there on day one, so I think the shield is related to the murder."

"It causes me discomfort to speak to you," Destroyer announced. "Emperors don't allow discomfort. If I have news, I will relay it through lesser creatures."

I didn't know who he considered lesser, but I didn't want anyone to be forced to endure it for me. "Do we need Roy?" I asked Mark.

"He can stay outside with Lance, or he can go searching for clues." Mark looked at Roy and gave him a signal.

"Okay, we can't put this off any longer," I said. "Let's hope we get the answers we need."

THE CHALETS WERE empty this session of the training so I suggested we use one as an interrogation room. They were small and easy to protect. Damping wards could keep everything confidential.

"I'll bring chairs," Mark said as he peeled off to the tents.

I unlocked the closest chalet and sent a clearing spell inside to freshen the air. Three chairs would fit around the central pit, but no table. Part of me thought that was good and would relax our subject, and the bigger part wanted something between me and a killer.

Mark towed three chairs in and we placed them around the raised area. Ravi would sit on the far side, Mark and I on either side of the door. There wasn't room to do much else, so maybe he wouldn't notice we'd trapped him.

"I ran into Ravi," Mark said. He was standing beside the open door. "He'll be here soon. I hate this in so many ways. Murder is bad enough, but with so few protectors we need you training them. Someone is going to try to shut you down any day."

"I'm sure the council is getting antsy," I said. "We'll deal with that when it happens. Two protectors are hard to push around." Well Mrs. V was hard to push around; I'd have to work on it. On this, I would call on my inner Mrs. V.

Ravi took the seat we'd set up and looked around the interior of the chalet. "This is a great place for experimenting. I could set up racks and watch samples as they develop."

"That was the original purpose," I said. Easing into the questions might help. Okay, maybe just me, but I wasn't going to jump all over him with accusations. "I'm not sure how I'll use them for training."

"Fill the center pit," Ravi said. "Not permanently. With a cover that can be removed." He stood and walked to the wall, touching it as if he was testing the material. "Nice neutral wood. Good wards."

"We need to ask for clarification," Mark said bringing us back to the topic. "There are some... holes in your background."

"You investigated me." Ravi returned to his chair. "I suppose it's to be expected. I didn't kill Magda, but you only have my word for it."

"Your university records. There are things there we should have known when you applied." I waited for him to get all fired up about violating his privacy, but he just smiled.

"If Samuel or Jasper are killers, it seems you need to be more stringent. I can't imagine protectors get to kill people."

This was a weird side of him. I expected resentment, or overly helpful, but not this superior attitude.

"We are changing the requirements," I said. "May I scan you?"

A spike of acid green fear flicked from his aura. It didn't feel like he was afraid, but I didn't know how else to interpret it. I wouldn't compel him—yet. I waited for his answer. Mark trusted me, even if I was a little confused why I was asking.

"Yes." The word came out so fast it felt forced.

"Close your eyes," I said. "It won't hurt. I promise. It's easier for me to work if you aren't watching." Not quite a lie. I just preferred not to see the anger in their eyes as witches realized how bare they were to me.

Ravi took a deep cleansing breath and relaxed in the chair then closed his eyes. I felt his normal barriers fade, but something still blocked me.

I formed my power into a needle to slide through the wall. That's how I thought of the technique. Most witches from the mainland had difficulty dropping illusions. Being around plain humans gave them cause to hold tight.

"It's okay," I said. "Only a minute more."

My power slipped in and I saw what Ravi was hiding from the world. Not the facts, but the emotions around them. He worried about the effects of keeping us hidden from the plain humans. That we could heal so much of the damage they did. He had a core of determination to keep us hidden. That must cause him pain. Ravi wasn't going to expose us. I felt some of that conflict myself.

It would be so much easier if I could read his murderous potential in his emotions, but no. Anger, maybe enough. I wasn't scanning for that, anyway. I spread my power out and found what I suspected. I withdrew.

"Mark and I will be right back," I said.

Outside, I checked the damping spell. Ravi wouldn't hear us, and no one was nearby.

"What?" Mark asked. "I didn't get any lies from him. The 'I didn't kill Magda' part? He believed it."

"Someone put a spell around him," I said. "Ravi isn't that kind of snotty witch. Like he knows more than anyone in the room."

"So everything could be a lie?" Mark gritted his teeth in frustration. "How complicated can this get. So we need to find the charm? Ask who gave it to him? Question him again when the spell is removed?"

"Let's try. It should be easy to release. I can't guarantee he'll remember when it happened."

Ravi was alert when we went back in. "You found something?"

I explained the results of my scan and he started pulling out the contents of his pockets.

"It will be something you got in the last few hours," Mark said.

Ravi held up a river stone. It was mostly the usual gray, but across the center was a deep red vein. "I found this on my walk."

Mark put the stone in an evidence bag spelled to suppress any magic. As soon as it was inside, Ravi gasped. "I didn't notice. I was being quite disrespectful. I apologize."

I waved away his concern. "Let's get back to the questions."

Mark took over and started with the activism notes. "None of it was available to us before. Why did you keep this secret?"

"I knew it was wrong." Ravi brushed his hair back from his forehead. "I was young and passionate. That instructor did me the biggest favor by setting the rules. I almost got involved in a bunch of actions I wouldn't be able to turn back from."

All truth. I listened to the rest of the questions with only half my attention. That charm could have affected anyone. Whoever placed it there must have known Ravi would see it and feel compelled to take it. The list of witches who fit that description could be the entire island.

13

Ravi sent Jasper to join us in the chalet. I didn't care if he told Jasper that it was an interrogation. Surprise only worked once.

"I don't think Ravi is our killer," Mark said. "If he was involved, it was because someone was controlling him."

That was too familiar. "I worried about the magic. First we have this weird shield that Mrs. V can't just lift. And now Ravi. How are we ever going to be sure?" Solving crimes had been easier when we didn't know people were being controlled.

"We're on alert and maybe the killer knows we released the spell. They'll be more careful. Maybe hold back on any spells for now."

Too much speculation. Jasper stepped into the chalet before we could explore the subject more. "You have a lead?"

His question caught me off guard. I expected curiosity, or anger. Not a feeling like I was a student sitting an exam and not getting an answer.

"We have more questions," Mark said. "Just sit, it won't take long."

He looked at me like we had a plan. We didn't. I realized what he was suggesting. "I'd like your permission to scan you."

"Why?" He wasn't going to make this easy.

"The protector doesn't need to justify," Mark said. I could tell he was reacting to the resentment and pain Jasper seemed to radiate without knowing.

"I won't compel you," I said. "We've learned some things that are worrying. Have you picked up any charms since you arrived?"

"No. Are you saying someone is forcing witches to commit murder?"

"We can't tell you details," Mark said. "Cossi can find the answer by scanning. If you refuse, it will take much longer."

Jasper took time to decide. His shields were down. I could just slip in and check, but I felt a wave of nausea at the thought. This wasn't a protector situation.

"I didn't do it," Jasper said. "You can tell if that's a lie, right?"

"If you believe it to be true, my power won't know. If Cossi reads uncertainty in your emotions, I can't ignore it."

His emotions were a mess. Grief, anger, guilt. All normal in someone who'd lost their partner. Also fairly normal if they'd killed a stranger and weren't a sociopath.

"I've been through this," Jasper said. "Not the scan, but the interrogation. I was there when my wife died. I was the main suspect when the local police found tampering. If I agree to the scan, will you know I'm not the killer? Is that why we need more protectors? To catch criminals?"

The answer was no, sort of. "Protectors are responsible for keeping the magical world protected," I said. "You know this. So I can't answer your question more than if there are more murders, the protectors will be solving crimes."

He digested that.

I felt Mark shift beside me. The dissonance of Jaspers feelings making him impatient. I touched his knee and shook my head. Pressing was the wrong tactic.

Over the next few minutes, I saw Jasper take control. It was rigid and protective, not natural. No matter what happened, he needed help and I'd get Doc Rene to work with him to heal the trauma.

"Fine." Jasper's answer wasn't acceptance. He sat straighter and crossed his arms. The decision came from a desire to get it over with, not to resolve the case.

"If you relax it will be easier on both of us," I said.

"That might be too much for me."

I stood and dragged my chair next to his. "May I touch you? It will help me through the surface."

He held out his hand, and I grasped it. I closed my eyes this time. The roil of colors was too distracting. I felt the urge to heal him, or start the process, but I was here for information.

I slipped inside his defenses. Behind the rage was what I wanted in a protector. His empathy and strength. Emotions that would support healing. He couldn't be our killer. I'd believe it if Magda's death was caused by rage, but the killer planned the death.

He could have been manipulated, and somehow his rage was being reinforced. I lingered trying to think of a way to help him. Nothing came to me. Protectors weren't omnipotent, he needed a healer.

I withdrew and took my seat back to Mark. "Nothing. Jasper, I need to ask questions. Please think before you answer." If he was being manipulated, perhaps he'd notice if he focused.

"Fine." He liked that word.

"I know you are still grieving. No one needs power to see you are in pain. But think back to before you arrived. Is there a change?"

He glared at me. I saw guilt again.

"I was clearer before. I don't need to think deeply about that. I want to be a protector. I passed the qualifications. I could see a future."

He sighed and paused for a moment.

"Something about Henbane is bringing it all back. From the moment I joined the other students on the boat to come here, I've been angry. The healer said recovery is not a straight line, so I didn't question it."

Mark stood and walked over to Jasper. "Do you have new wounds, or marks? Is it possible you've been hexed?"

Jasper pushed up his sleeves. His arms were covered in scars and healed burns. "I'm a blacksmith. Who knows."

"One more thing," Mark said. "We have information that you ordered a number of items that cause us concern."

Jasper rolled his eyes. It was a relief to see such a normal reaction.

"You mean the combat stuff?"

"You can understand why I need to know your reasoning." Mark waited for Jasper to answer.

"Stupid of me. I went on the plain human internet. I read some stuff about learning to defend myself would make me feel better. I didn't even try the lessons that came with it. Maybe that was when I realized my work with the healer was helping."

"Thanks you. Go back to your room," Mark said. "Send Samuel down, please."

Jasper didn't ask if we thought he was innocent. He stalked through the door, holding his anger and embarrassment in check.

"He needs Doc Rene," Mark said. "No doubt about his reasoning, but if he was that aware a few months ago, something is definitely wrong."

"I'll call her. I think you're right. Someone is keeping him in pain."

I stepped outside the chalet and walked around the back. If Samuel came while I was talking, I didn't want to be interrupted.

"What's the emergency?" Doc Rene asked instead of saying hi. I checked the time. Almost midnight.

"Sorry, no crisis. I need to ask you about Jasper. He needs help."

"When I tested him in the screening, he was on his way to healed. What do you know about grief?"

"Jasper said it's not a straight line. I don't really know much. I was sad when my parents died but not like him."

"Some people feel more than others, especially witches with empathy, or some other kind of power like it. He's right even years after the incident, a wave can hit. But there's a point where the time between the waves gets longer. He was there. Why?"

I told her what I saw in the scan. "We're going deeper on all the students trying to find a clue."

"Not normal. You need me to come right away?" I heard rustling in the background. She was getting dressed.

"I don't know. Do you think it's that urgent?"

"No time better. Even if I just help him sleep better. I'll be there in twenty."

14

————

Doc Rene agreed to meet me at the chalet. If nothing changed, our interrogation of Samuel would be at an end by the time she arrived.

As I returned to the chalet door, I noticed Samuel leave the main building and head my way. I told Mark and waited at the door. I didn't feel anything like fear and that was a bit odd. I mean, we didn't really think either Jasper or Ravi were our killer, so it was highly likely Samuel murdered Magda. I should be worried.

"Happy to help," Samuel said as I waved him inside. "Hear you're trying to eliminate the obvious suspects. Good. It will allow you to focus on the culprit and you can start our training again."

Mark told him to sit and then closed the door. Samuel smiled and sat a little slouched and fully relaxed. He was the only who didn't feel damaged. Still covered by a smooth shield that hid his full emotional range.

"We have a little more information," Mark said.

I'd expected him to start with the scan, but I didn't say anything. I guess if I was going in past that wall, knowing the reason he didn't seem to exist before six years ago would help. My inner voice said that was wrong, but not what I should do about it. Samuel, all the students, lived in the plain human world. It might be normal to hide everything.

"Ask away," Samuel said. "I have nothing to hide."

That was a lie. I felt Mark twitch bedside me. His power knew it too. But everyone lies all the time.

"Why is there no evidence of you until six years ago?" Mark pretended to check his notes. "No social media, plain or magic. Really nothing we can find until after you graduated university."

A flicker of annoyance in his aura surprised me. He was so controlled normally. I kept my eyes on him and waited for his answer.

Eventually he must have decided we'd win the waiting game.

"As you can imagine, my family being so wealthy and important in our world are careful about their privacy." He unslouched and leaned forward. "It took me years to believe I wouldn't be a target if I lived a little more publicly."

Another lie.

"I would expect to find school records," Mark said. "You know a tech witch can get past any firewalls."

"I had private tutors," he said. "When I went into higher learning, a plain university, my parents paid to have my records removed after graduation. It's not like we check that type of thing. Plain humans need to prove they attended a prestigious institute. We have other means."

"Can you give us some background on your time there?" Mark asked.

"I can check with the family. Perhaps the records were not destroyed."

A gray tinge made it through the shield. We were

annoying him with our questions. I suppose it might be because he wasn't used to being questioned. Or were we getting too close to discovering he killed Magda? I threw that away before the thought pushed me to skew the questions.

"Have you felt anything change in the days since you arrived," I asked. Like Mark, I didn't want to scan him until later.

"Changed? Have the other students mentioned a shift?" His caring look was back and his emotions behind his ward.

"Cossi asked if you felt anything?" Mark said.

"I'm not sure. I mean, it's all a little disconcerting to be on Henbane and not need to worry about making a mistake. And a murder. I suppose I feel a bit more worried. Is that the kind of thing?"

"Any new charms, or spells?" Mark asked.

"Is someone on Henbane using harmful magic?" Samuel asked, his surprise was genuine. "Or, is it a test. A protector should see the harm, right?"

I took his answers as a no. I also made a note for future classes to create a test like this. Not harmful, but to see if the student could identify harm.

"Have you noticed the shield?" I asked. "Around the retreat?"

"No. Is there one? Oh, does that explain the stifling feeling?" He shook his head. "If that's right, then someone needs more instruction in shielding. Perhaps a youngster? Testing boundaries?"

Not quite the truth. What was going on with him?

"I'd like to scan you," I said. I still felt reluctant to touch his smooth shell, let alone punch through it. "I won't tell what I find."

"You mean unless you find I'm capable of murder?"

I chose not to answer. He kept slipping past giving us information that would clear his name. This time I wouldn't bite at the misdirection. The silence this time was heavy. I missed the sound of wildlife. The chatter in my head from animals in the area. Destroyer's pronouncements.

Before Samuel deigned to give permission, or deny it, we were disturbed by a knock on the door.

Doc Rene had arrived. "Which room?" I guess she didn't want to waste time with small talk.

I stepped out and closed the door. "Second floor the Wave room. About halfway down the hall. I'll show you."

"No. I can find it. I want to be alone with my patient. Does he know I'm coming?"

"I can send him a text," I said digging my phone out of my pocket.

She put her hand on mine to stop me. "I don't want him to have notice. He'll take measures to avoid me. Do you want an update when I leave?"

Of course I did. Was the offer real? I didn't think she'd keep anything critical from me. "You can decide. I'll be in my suite, or here depending on how long it takes."

"Anything else I should know? From your interrogation?" She must have seen the guilt flash across my face because she chuckled. "What did we say about taking on responsibility for everything?"

"It would kill me. We didn't cause his pain. Okay. On thing we found from both Ravi and Jasper that might be important is that something changed when they got here. Ravi had a charmed stone. Jasper said his grief increased when he was on his way with the others. He doesn't have a charm."

"But you think he's been what? Hexed?"

"No. I can recognize that. Maybe it's nothing, but spells can be cast with just a touch."

She hiked her medical bag higher on her shoulder and nodded. "My job is to heal him. I won't go looking for clues."

"I know. To be honest, I think he's innocent and maybe should have taken more time to heal before he came."

"When we've solved this case, we need to deal with how a murderer got through the screening if it's one of the students. But for now, you find the killer, and I'll heal the wounds."

15

———

When I joined Mark and Samuel again, the room was zinging with discomfort. If Mark continued to question Samuel in my absence, he'd hit a sore point.

"What did I miss?" I kept my voice light, hoping the buzz of annoyance was just the result of silence.

"Who was that?" Samuel asked. "I thought this was important. If you are happy to interrupt this, I can come back."

He was half right. I should have sent the details to Doc Rene by text. Leaving to help Jasper gave Samuel time to come up with another tactic. "Are you ready to be scanned?"

He stared me down like Mark wasn't in the room. No matter the outcome, this witch wasn't a good candidate for protector.

"If you are reluctant to allow a protector to scan you, how will you convince another witch to allow you in?" Mark asked following the same thought process.

"Do protectors commonly scan people? Samuel wasn't backing down.

I'd force him if needed. Doing that felt like failure. What confused me was he hadn't said no. "We don't use it often. Or we haven't in the past. Why are you having so much difficulty with the question?"

He sagged. "My family. We kept everything private. I find myself torn. The son of the Whitlock family is fighting decades of training. The budding protector wants to agree. I suppose I must say yes and clear my name. Go ahead."

Everything about him was giving off the same feelings of lies and not lies. I felt like my previous experience hadn't set me up for success. "Please don't fight me. It will hurt you and me."

My first attempt hit a solid wall. It felt slippery and firm. When I pushed it bent. "Can you remove the barrier?"

"What barrier?"

If this was imposed, I had no choice. I didn't warn him because it would make it harder. I tried to think of a real life thing that felt the same as his wall. Yes, a wet suit. A heavy duty one if that existed. I withdrew enough to check my phone. A quick search didn't help. I needed a hard surface to stop it bending as I cut.

This wasn't actually neoprene, though. Worth a try. I imagined my power as an Xacto knife. Poking didn't work but a fast slash had his shield peeling back.

Inside his emotions were curled around each other. Pain, fear, hope. His parents hadn't just taught him to be careful they'd built a wall of fear. I explained his protective wall. They'd blocked him from accessing anything of the real world.

I withdrew quickly, no wiser about his guilt.

"Thanks. You can go back to your room," I said.

I expected to get an objection, or a slew of questions

about what I found. But he stood and walked past us without any reaction.

When we were alone, Mark placed a privacy ward inside to allow us to talk.

"So?"

"What happened while I was gone?" If I hoped to analyze the results of the scan, I needed context.

"He sat there," Mark said pointing at the chair. "Like he was meditating. Like I wasn't here."

"What did your power tell you about the truth?"

"That was odd. Usually I can sense a difference between lying because they know the truth and lying because they believe a lie. This time it was muddy, everything was both a lie and the truth. But none of it was because he'd bought a lie."

"Same here. I found nothing inside his wall that told me he murdered Magda. He's hurt and I don't think he can access it. I'm sending him home when we solve the case." I hoped his current home was not with his family. "He needs help but I'm not weighing Doc Rene down with all the student problems."

"We'll figure it out," Mark said. "We didn't find the killer, but we crossed things off the list, and we got Jasper help. Let's call it a night."

We left the chairs in place in case we needed to interrogate another suspect—not sure where we were going to find one. Mark released all the wards and we stepped outside.

Lance was waiting there with Roy and Destroyer.

"What happened?" The words were out of my mouth before the change registered.

"The shield is gone," Mark said. "Do you know when?"

"Crows do not tell time," Destroyer said almost making me miss the answer.

"About ten minutes ago," Lance said. "I came to make sure you were all okay. These two seemed upset."

Destroyer gave out a very non-imperial caw. "Emperors do not get upset. I was exploring when I heard your thoughts again."

"The crow is lying," Roy said to me. "I'm glad we can get through here again."

Hard as it was to balance so many voices in my head with the ones from Lance and Mark, I tried to sort things out.

"That makes it when I was scanning Samuel. Mark, did you notice anything that would explain it?"

"No, but our wards might explain that. I'll text D and Mrs. V to let them know. Maybe she can find a trace of what released it."

I didn't hold out much hope. Once magic was gone, there was no evidence. Not like on cop shows where some strand of hair points directly to the perp. Spells were active or gone.

"Another clue that doesn't lead anywhere," I said. "Maybe we're just tired. I'll check with Doc Rene and then I need sleep. We'll come at it again in the morning. Now the animals can get in, I expect they'll be sniffing around in the hopes of free muffins."

We said our goodnights, and I headed to the main room. Doc Rene's bike was still in the parking spot, so she hadn't finished with Jasper. If she was still working with him, I'd leave a note outside his door asking her to pop by and tell me what progress she'd made.

I made a sleep tea and headed upstairs. Doc Rene was on her way down.

"I can make you some tea," I said. "I'm pretty sure we have a few cookies as well."

"Thanks, I'll take you up on that."

Doc Rene followed me to the kitchen/ common room. I turned the kettle on and found a handful of apricot thumb print cookies in the jar. The Inner Spell was only a few minutes ride from the Earth Witch village and we often got the benefit of someone's baking efforts.

When the tea was ready, we sat at the end of the refectory table to talk. I set a warming spell on my tea because I couldn't risk sipping at it and falling asleep while she talked.

"First, Jasper is sleeping. He'll be fine in the morning," she said. "Well, fine is probably a stretch, but there was something pushing him deeper into the pain."

"So like the other two, he had some kind of spell." Ravi was the only one with a physical object, but Samuel admitted to feeling anxiety he wasn't used to. And now something had spiked Jasper's grief.

"I was able to remove the spell," Doc Rene said. "It took work but now he'll rest and recover."

"How long ago?" I knew the answer before she told me.

"By now? About half an hour. Why?"

The same time the shield lifted "I have a theory. Do you have time to help me think it through?"

She took another cookie and gestured for me to continue.

"There was a shield around the retreat," I said then filled her in on the effects. "You broke through the block for Jasper, I scanned Samuel and the shield disappeared all about the same time."

"You think it's all tied to the wards? It could be," she said. "What about Ravi. You said he had a charm. That couldn't have been at exactly the same."

"That's a good point, except we didn't deactivate it, just took it. Mark can check to see if the spell is gone."

"Now we just have to figure out how to prove the events are linked to the murder, and who made it all happen." I couldn't believe such a big clue was going to fizzle out like every discovery we made.

"I am sorry, Cossi," Doc Rene said. She sent her mug to the sink and took the last cookie from the plate. "It feels like I didn't even bother to screen these people. None of them should be your first students."

It wasn't her fault. I knew a bit about taking on responsibility for mistakes I didn't make. "We did our best. And it looks like the people we screened probably were good candidates until they were manipulated."

"You're kind to say that. I've been thinking though. We need to be more... I don't know, diligent isn't the right word. We need to screen deeper before qualifying people and then re-screen when they arrive? Does that make sense?"

We could apply more stringent tests, but what if no one passed? "There are holes in our non-power tests too. The murder takes priority and then continuing the training for the students. But we'll debrief when it's over. We're too close right now to change anything."

She sent the plate to the sink and grabbed her bag. "I'll check on Jasper tomorrow. Get some sleep before I have to intervene on your health."

16

The next morning didn't bring any revelations. All I had was waiting. For Mrs. V to find any clues about the shield, unlikely or the stone Ravi found —more likely. For D to find something in his background research to point us to the killer. For Mark to check with his colleagues.

Doc Rene checked on Jasper early and pronounced him ready to resume, I messaged everyone to come to the common room for today's lessons. It would be the kind of theory lecture that in plain schools came with several well-researched trains of thought. I guess we were building that for protector training.

When we were seated around the refectory table with drinks and snacks, I gave them an update on what happened. No the secrets I found in the scan, that was private. But the charms, the shield. "We're going to focus back on our training. The investigation is currently in other hands."

"But you don't know who the killer is?" Ravi asked. "Is

that usual? I know you've solved murders before. I hope it's not what we're expected to do."

"There isn't a usual in any of what we do," I said. It had been silly of me to think the murder could be put behind us. "And I hope we don't become experts at catching killers. IT's a good place to start. Why do you think a protector would need to be involved in a criminal case?"

"Perhaps this is not a concern on Henbane," Samuel said with wave of his hand. "Those of us who live in the wider world would see it as a danger. If a plain human stumbled on a witch's body—or a shifters' I suppose, we might lose our protection."

"True, but Henbane isn't the only hidden community. So it's more global than a big city problem," Ravi said. "I can't think of a single murder in my lifetime until recently. Is it because a change like that is a precursor of a bigger problem?"

I didn't answer because I had no idea. I was compelled to help solve murders, but I didn't know that they were a recent phenomenon.

"It makes sense to me," Jasper said. "If our job is to protect the magical world, wouldn't everything be our job?"

"We can't do everything," Ravi said. "And look at us, we all have completely different focuses. Not just us, Cossi too. And Mrs. V. If there was a single reason for a protector to exist, we would have the same interests, right?"

"That's a pretty simplistic view," Samuel said. "How did you change when you became the protector, Cossi?"

I guess I was a good example because the other protectors didn't suddenly find out they were witches in their early twenties. So what had changed?

"Mrs. V suspected I was changing," I said, thinking through the events while I spoke. "You know I didn't have a normal childhood for a witch. And this school is training you not making you natural protectors."

"Yes, we accept all the qualifying facts," Samuel said. "Just tell us and we can figure it out."

"You should be more respectful," Jasper said. "Cossi is doing her best to teach us."

The between the two affected Ravi, who was pressing his lips together to avoid weighing in. There was no color of emotion just a tingle of annoyance. I made an effort not to react.

"It's fine. This must be frustrating for all of you. I know it is for me. I can't turn away from the compulsion to train you. I have to trust my power. But this is really new. I hope we can be respectful of each other, but we need to feel safe to raise concerns."

I let that sink in for a beat before I started telling them my experience. "From the day I arrived, my powers went through, I guess the best way to describe it was an evolution. It took me months to find what my powers would do. Part of that was Phillip continuing to suppress me. Part of it was living as a plain human for so long." That was something I hadn't realized until now.

"So you got your powers a little at a time?" Jasper asked.

"No, the best example is my ability to read emotions. It started with seeing color and knowing what it stood for. Then started to smell them. Believe me that wasn't always pleasant. Then taste came along. Using those senses, I read the shades of emotion pretty clearly. Nothing changed when we realized I was a protector."

"Did anything?" Samuel asked. "I mean if there isn't a protector power then why are you one and not someone else."

"Why would you ask that?" Ravi snapped the words out. "It's like asking Mark what makes him a police witch?"

"Why not. None of us have a specialty. I mean Jasper can work metal, but he doesn't need to."

"You don't know what I need," Jasper said. "What's your specialty?"

The stress built again. Why was today bringing out the antagonism? "Samuel's question is right. Mark is compelled by his powers to investigate and maintain order, so he wouldn't use his powers for anything else."

"Did we get chosen because we had no compulsion?" Jasper asked.

"That wasn't a screening factor. I'm not the only one who believes there's a guiding something, right?"

"The universe, yes," Ravi said. "Everyone knows fate makes choices."

"You didn't answer my question," Samuel said.

"I got what I think of as a power up." I remembered the test of forcing Phillip to tell the truth. "And a limit." I told them how my normal power wouldn't force the truth because it wasn't a threat to the world, but when I asked about the community, the power up kicked in.

"So you could just go around the island using that skill demanding if people are the murderer?" Ravi asked the question, but all three suddenly focused on me.

"No. I don't see that working. We need to find the killer first."

This wasn't going in the direction I'd hoped. Was I useless in managing a discussion?

"Why aren't protectors being born?" Jasper asked. "I mean if we need more, why isn't the universe making them?"

"I have no answer. I know the few we have can't cover the

world. Mrs. V agrees. Maybe we're reacting to the small signs before the problem gets big enough? It's not like we can ask the universe."

I pushed them back on the lesson; what are the real threats to our world?

THE DISCUSSION WAS PRETTY GOOD. We came up with scenarios that might require a protector. Concerns like the community relying on a protector if there were enough and not solving their own problems. The animosity spiked a couple of times, but never derailed us for long.

"I think that's enough for today," I said. "You should go explore the island a little more."

"Something occurs to me," Samuel said. "What if you are wrong about your need to make more protectors. That the urge is more about one of you going into the world? I mean why does Henbane need one resident protector let alone two?"

I saw the shock rising from Ravi and Jasper. They didn't like him questioning me. I spoke before an argument could break out. "I can't explain it but we're not wrong. I may end up traveling, but Henbane is my home. But you have more to ask, right?"

"What if Magda's murder was to stop you?"

"You mean the motive? Or the universe jealous of me doing my job?"

A spear of surprise reached for me before Samuel regained his control. "Either?"

"Like I said, we can't ask the universe. I can't imagine my need to train witches affects it. And you may be right. We won't know the motive until we've uncovered the killer."

17

I wasn't the best at sitting and waiting, but there was nothing else to do. I was the only person on the investigation who didn't have a specific job. I guess that just adds to the argument that protectors aren't supposed to be investigators.

While the students filled their time, I enjoyed the sound of the real world. Now the animals were allowed in, I heard the birds chirping, the squirrels bickering, and the occasional imperial muttering from Destroyer. Every muscle in my body relaxed after being on alert for the last few days.

It didn't feel like we were close to solving the murder, but what I'd been missing was hope. I knew we'd be successful. It might take longer than I liked, but we would catch Magda's killer.

Late in the afternoon, D arrived. "I found something. Mark's on his way. We need to decide how to deal with it."

"What?" I wasn't surprised that Mrs. V didn't join us. In the past we hadn't included her.

"Wait until he gets here. I want everyone on the same

page. You have any food around?" He dropped his laptop on the table and started digging through the cupboards.

"We'll go into my suite," I said. "When Mark gets here. This is too public. And yes, there's sandwich stuff in the fridge. We can make a platter while we wait."

Putting a meal together gave me something to do and meant I didn't pester D to tell me the details, or give me a hint. Sheena would be dropping off the evening meal, so my students wouldn't need any of the supplies.

I heard Roy before I saw Mark. "Feels better here. No so much like dead."

Mark joined us and I led them to my private quarters. I didn't think of it as an apartment. The main building was looking more and more like a hotel and so I felt like I had a permanent hotel suite. I did miss the apartment over the bookstore, but being on site was more important.

We settled in and D flipped open his laptop. After a bite of his sandwich, he said, "Samuel isn't the only one with a questionable background."

"Just tell us what you found," Mark said. "I appreciate the break, but I have calls to make."

"Magda Potter wasn't always Magda Potter," D said. "She changed her name seven years ago. Before that, she was Magda Erikson."

"People change names for all kinds of reasons," I said. "That doesn't necessarily mean anything. If it was serious surely she'd change her first name too."

"She was involved in a public dispute about historical records—specifically, whether certain documents should be made accessible to researchers or kept sealed due to sensitive personal information."

"That doesn't sound bad enough to change your identity.

Scholars argue all the time. Even in the plain world." I wanted to tell him to stop stringing it out, but D wasn't into drama so there was a reason.

"Family histories, magical lineages, records of magical crimes and punishments from the early days of witches settling in the area." He took another bite. I wondered when he'd last eaten. "Magda was teaching at the time and argued that the documents should remain sealed to protect the privacy of descendants. Someone else argued they should be public for historical research purposes. I mean not public public, but for us anyway."

"Who?" Mark asked. "Another suspect?"

"Zinnia Flor," D said, pointing to his screen as if we could read it. "She was working on her master's thesis about historical documentation preservation techniques. Real paper stuff because nothing had been imaged. She and Magda didn't keep it to the usual passive aggressive sniping that academics use. Lots of yelling and name calling. The university sided with Zinnia. Magda left."

"What university?" I had very little knowledge of the magical scholarly world.

"Dreven, it's outside Winnipeg," D said. "No plain humans nearby, don't worry."

I felt a chill. Zinnia was my friend. We'd shared meals, discussed magical theory, laughed about the challenges of integrating into a new community. She'd managed The Inner Spell when it was a retreat. She'd never once mentioned knowing Magda in all the times I'd talked about my new students.

"She's been here for more than a year. We would have noticed if she was capable of this," I said.

"It's cute how you keep thinking that when reality shows

you differently," Mark said. "None of the murderers you've found so far seemed like they would kill."

"I know. It's just that as a protector, shouldn't I have like a sense of people's intentions?"

"Maybe if a murder actually threatened our world?" D said.

"Zinnia's magic is focused on historical research and connections," I said. "Tracking how people and events relate to each other across time. Maybe Magda found something she missed. Tried to get revenge for the incident?"

"I don't know, but here's what I found." D pulled up more information. "After the conflict with Magda, Zinnia's academic career stalled. She didn't finish her thesis, didn't get her degree, worked a series of temporary research positions. Every reference I can find describes her as brilliant but difficult or talented but holds grudges."

"Lots of people are difficult and hold grudges without being murderers," I said, defending her even though doubt was creeping in.

"True," Mark said. "But Zinnia it might be enough for motive. If her career was so important to her."

"I'll talk to her," I said. "She's my friend and I owe her that at least. Alone."

"That's too dangerous," Mark said. "If she killed Magda, she might try to do the same to you."

"I'll be on alert. Magda wasn't. You can be outside, but I am going in alone."

The team didn't like it, but they had no choice. D would be right outside and ready to give me a head up if someone tried to interrupt. Mark would wait with Destroyer and Roy ready to come to my aid. They both handed me defensive charms.

A half hour later I walked past the bookstore to the side

entrance. The store was closed because Lance was still in the forest on guard. The windows of the apartment were open, and the sound of Zinnia's favorite pop singer drifted out.

I sent her a text to expect me and headed up the stairs.

"Cossi!" she said, opening the door with a genuine smile. "I wasn't expecting you. Is everything okay with the training program? Do you need a book? Lance gave me the keys just in case."

"Can we talk?" I asked, settling into the chair across from her worktable. "It's about Magda Potter."

Something flickered across Zinnia's face—too quick to identify clearly, but enough to make my pulse quicken.

"The student who died?" she said carefully. "That's terrible. How are you holding up?"

"Did you know her?" I asked directly because there was no point in dancing around the topic.

Zinnia went very still. "Why would you ask that?"

"Because I found out that you and Magda had a professional conflict seven years ago. A public dispute that ended with her leaving the community and changing her name."

For a long moment, Zinnia didn't respond. Then she set down the document she'd been holding and met my eyes.

"Yes," she said quietly. "I knew her. Or I knew Magda Erikson, anyway. I didn't realize she'd changed her name until after she died."

Relief she hadn't tried to lie flooded me. "Why didn't you tell me you knew her when it happened?"

"Because I was afraid of exactly this," Zinnia said, gesturing between us. "I knew how it would look. Old conflict. I never mentioned knowing her. It looks suspicious."

"It is suspicious," I said.

"I know." Zinnia stood and began pacing. "But Cossi, I didn't kill her. That conflict was seven years ago. I was young and stupid and took an academic disagreement way too personally. Yes, it damaged my career. Yes, I resented her for a long time. But I moved past it. And frankly, the fact I behaved the way I did was a clear sign I wasn't cut out for academia."

"Is that why you were so happy to settle here? To get involved with the project?" She'd stepped in and joined a committee trying to solve a problem of plain humans and selfies and wards.

"Yes. Because this island seemed like a good place to rebuild my career and my life. I can freelance from here and everyone is a witch or a shifter. I fit here." She stopped pacing and looked at me. "I didn't stay because I thought Magda would ever come. Did you think I was hunting down someone I had a fight with seven years ago."

The emotions all read as proof she was innocent. Was that enough to dismiss her from our suspect list? Or was my friendship confusing my perception?

"Did you come to The Inner Spell?" I asked.

"Early on I walked by it a few times. I was curious about what you were building. But when the students arrived, I thought you wouldn't want distractions. And I didn't know Magda was there until I heard she died."

"I want to believe you," I said. "Our friendship is important to me. Will you let me scan you?"

She sat and placed her hands on her knees. "Go ahead. You can tell if someone is lying. I didn't kill her. But look inside to see if I even wanted to."

I wanted to cry. How would our friendship survive this violation? I reached out with my powers. She had no barriers. Everything she showed to the world was reflected inside. Hope, curiosity, fun. Not even a trace of malice or vengeance.

Before I could respond, my phone buzzed with an urgent text from D: *Samuel just arrived outside the door. He's coming up.*

18

Wwhat the heck did he want? If my students think they can follow me around and interrupt me, I was going to put some boundaries in place, not just normal ones either.

"Do you know why Samuel Whitlock is here?" Was she hiding something else?

"No," Zinnia said, looking confused. "Although, I guess I know who he is from your piece in the community newsletter. But why do you ask?"

"He's here."

A knock at the door interrupted us before I could say anything else. Zinnia opened it and Samuel stood there with his usual helpful smile and casual attitude.

"Sorry to interrupt," he said, looking between us. "I was taking a walk and saw Cossi come in. I wanted to make sure everything was okay—given the recent tensions, I've been worried about everyone's safety."

Our safety wasn't his concern, but saying that would probably be the wrong thing. If I wanted him to be open and honest, I couldn't chastise him.

"Everything's fine," I said. "We were just talking. I visit my friends all the time."

"About Magda's death?" Samuel asked. His tone was sympathetic, but his eyes were sharp. "I know her death has been difficult for everyone. If there's anything I can do to help with the investigation or support the team... I'm sure all of us want to get on with things."

I couldn't get a handle on him. Even after our interrogation and my scan he seemed too polished. Too curious.

"No need," I said. "You are here to learn protector skills. I know the investigation is getting in the way of our planned lessons, but your priority is still to learn."

"Of course. I have noticed the bookstore isn't opening. Is there a way to purchase, or browse?"

"I have the key," Zinnia said. "I'll let you in and wait while you choose."

Samuel stepped aside to let her pass. Zinnia led us down the stairs, pausing to lock her apartment. I was relieved for some reason that she didn't take the shortcut through the other stairway directly into the store.

We split up as soon as we were outside. She took Samuel to the bookstore. I waited until they were out of sight before I sent my group text.

Meet in Jan's.

Both Mark and D sent a thumbs up. Mrs. V told us to send her an update.

It only took me a few seconds to cross the street and enter the bistro. Mark followed and D was already sitting at a corner table, beers ready.

"We should have placed some charms around the place to record," he said. "I swear everyone is only telling the truth when we specifically ask. Holding back information if we don't. It's like dealing with a two-year-old."

If we couldn't believe anyone how would we solve the case? "We can't listen in on people. I can't say you're wrong either."

I took a deep drink of the wonderful hoppy beer and told them what I'd found out. And what Samuel gave as an excuse for barging in. "I believe Zinnia. Even if she's holding something back, she didn't kill Magda.

"I don't know if this makes a difference, but I found email correspondence between Magda and Zinnia from three weeks ago," D said. "They'd reconnected. Magda reached out to apologize for how their conflict ended and to say she regretted letting professional disagreement damage their relationship."

"What did Zinnia say I response?" I asked.

"She accepted the apology. Said she was glad to move past it. They made plans to have coffee and catch up." Pointed to a date on the screen. "The meeting was scheduled for two days after Magda died."

"I think we have better motives," Mark said. "We're missing something or not interpreting a fact correctly. Zinnia is off the hook as far as I'm concerned."

Now we could talk about the next event more clearly. "Samuel was very interested in what Zinnia and I were discussing," I said. "His offer of help and request to use the bookstore didn't hit me like he was lying, but I wasn't convinced. I think he's trying to keep tabs on the investigation."

"He's always offering to help out. Like he knows how to do anything better than another witch," D noted. "Showing up at convenient times to overhear conversations. If I'm not careful he pulls me off track on my task."

"Do you distracting us by pointing at other suspects?" Mark asked. "It doesn't have to be overt. But now he shows up when we're questioning Zinnia. Maybe we didn't notice him pushing Ravi or Jasper forward."

"I don't think he could do that to me," I said. "He might just think he's better than anyone. A lousy trait for a protector. I'm already thinking of sending him away when we're done here."

"And we don't have evidence more against Samuel than the others," Mark pointed out. "Suspicions about his behavior and concerns about his background. I can't tell the council to punish him without more proof."

"There is a difference," D said. "All that explaining about homeschooling and records being purged. I'll be happier when I find something to back up his story."

"We can't let this go on forever. It's putting the wrong attention on the training," I said. "Is there anything we can do to make more progress?"

All this frustration was so out of place in the bistro. The cold refreshing beer, the aroma of roasting meat and vegetables wafting from the kitchen. The murmur of the other patrons as they swapped stories. This was all a warm and comforting blanket. Our discussion was like throwing ice down the back of my neck.

"Jasper is in Doc Rene's hands," D said. "She doesn't think he would kill anyone. I'm expecting a call about Ravi from one of my contacts. There is one step we haven't talked about."

If we'd dismissed our concerns for two of our four suspects, that was a big leap forward. "What step?"

"Talking to the Whitmores," he said. "Before you freak out. I know they are powerful and very protective of their privacy—like they are hiding something. But we have two protectors on our side. They can't deny Mrs. V's request for a meeting."

"Does the power work over a video call?" Mark asked. "I know you've both done protector work that way, but did you need to use your power?"

I should have experimented. Like a lot of things under the 'should have' column, I didn't spend time on it. "I've used it over the phone. Or, at least, I've read emotions that way. Do you really think we'll have to compel them?"

"Should and reality is not always the same thing," Mark said. "A protector asking should be enough."

"It's not the only way," Mark said. "And who says we only do one plan at a time? We could set a trap."

I liked that idea better. I didn't care for the little voice calling me a coward. A trap would get us the answers right away. "What do we have to bait it?"

"I'll find something," Mark said. "I'll bet Destroyer has some ideas too."

19

W e agreed to split up for an hour. Not to go back to The Inner Spell, but to figure out what we needed. D volunteered to get Mrs. V's input and, since only I could hear him, I promised to bring back anything Destroy came up with—minus the imperial padding.

Mark told us he had a couple of people to visit and left D and I at Jan's.

"Mrs. V is ready," D said. "I guess I'll head there now."

"Remember to get your own ideas on the table," I said. "Mrs. V might not have the only solution." He tended to defer to her, and me I suppose, when the topic was outside his expertise.

"Maybe I'll come up with some on the way over," he said. "I'm still half convinced it's not one of the students."

He left, and I went to the bar to order lunch. Jan's was as good a place as any to chat with Destroyer. "What's the special?" The aroma must have magic in it to lure in hungry diners.

"Something new," Jan said. "Now Marcus is in school,

and has made friends, he just sends me ideas. So we have something I never thought I'd do. It's vegan."

"It smells like roast beef with all the trimmings." I hoped it wasn't some badly flavored tofu. The main issue with vegan food made to replace omnivore food was how much processing it went through.

"It's Henbane, magic." Jan called my order back and drew me another pint of beer. "We can't put market box together for the plain customers, but I'm hoping I can share some of the successful ones on my channel for us witches."

Jan was the kind of business owner who liked lots of streams of income. He sold weekly recipe packs on-line to magical and non-magical people. He had a beer and a cider club going with Lance. And apparently a magical streaming service.

"Can I bring Destroyer in?" I always like to get permission because not everyone enjoys a crow flying around their homes or businesses.

"Welcome any time. Shall I put out a saucer of beer?"

"Maybe later," I said remembering Destroyers lack of sense after drinking. "I'll be working with him, and I'll set a ward so no one can overhear."

"Keep that table. If you need me, just wave." He handed me my drink and headed to the kitchen to bring my food.

"You need to open the door," Destroyer said. "You should cast a spell on all door that makes them open when the emperor approaches."

Not likely. I ignored his response to my thoughts. I felt weird sitting with him and just thinking about our conversation. As soon as my food arrived, I cast the ward. "How much have you heard?"

I tested the vegan stew and almost fainted. This wasn't fake anything. To me it tasted like a roast beef stew that had been cooking for hours. My power sorted the reality from the magic. The spell acted on the diner's wants. Not like you are eating meat and we've fooled you, but in this is all vegan and you'll taste and feel it as meat if that's what you want.

Were we all about to change our dietary requirements?

"It is unlikely," Destroyer said. "Are you ready to make this plan or will you continue on the culinary path?"

I took another bite and thought, "go ahead tell me what you think." Talking aloud would come when my plate was clean.

"Now that the impertinent shield is removed, my spies can operate. Your suspects are not doing anything suspicious. I suggest you take them to the highest tree and make them speak the full truth."

Crows could be quite ferocious. "That won't be necessary. I need something more subtle and my preference is that the guilty party survive to face punishment."

"I thought you would say that. You have information that the students are not aware of. This is a good tactic and worthy of an emperor's familiar. You must trick them will illusion." He fluttered his wings and glanced at Jan. "I am thirsty."

He was onto something and my plate was empty. I waved at Jan and dropped the ward.

"I'll bring refreshments," he said as he took my plate. "Another beer?"

"I think I need to keep my head clear."

"I require beer," Destroyer announced.

"When we are finished. Water for now."

Jan laughed as though he'd read our conversation.

In a minute Destroyer had a saucer of water, I had a large coffee and the ward was in place.

"Do you have a trick in mind?" The basic idea was good,

but I worried an illusion would be a problem. Like it would give us false answers, or worse, ambiguous ones.

"You have them kept in your nest. I can give an order to one of my subjects to say they witnessed the murder." He sipped at the water and waited. Our link told me he didn't expect an argument.

"It might work," I said. "We can use the shield to explain why this witness waited to come forward."

"Do you prefer any prey animal?" He hopped to face Jan, expecting his reward.

"The problem is that only I can understand animals. How is it a trap if a squirrel is chittering at me and I interpret?"

"If you will not accept that I have the perfect plan, order my beer and leave."

He didn't have the right plan, but his trap made me think about a better one. And it was about time for us to meet up.

I dropped the ward and told Jan to give Destroyer one saucer of beer and nothing more.

"I'll let him out when he's finished. Did you work out your problem?"

"Almost. I think we'll be back to normal soon."

"I'll drop of the dinner supplies tonight."

I sent a text to the group. Time to decide. *Mrs. V's cottage in ten.*

I was the last to arrive. Mark's calls hadn't taken any time at all. Mrs. V told me to make tea and dig out Valerie's latest shortbread cookies. I brewed an alertness blend. If we did this right, it would be a long day.

"We have the beginnings of a plan," Mrs. V said. "It is possible we were under more influence than I found. Cossi, do you know why it's taken us so long to come to this idea?"

"No. And one of the questions we need to ask the killer is about that shield. How can someone do that? Create a spell that neither of us are able to undo?"

She looked at Tulip and said, "No we are not too trusting."

"Let's not get distracted," Mark said. "All these answers will come later. Ideas for the trap?"

No one took out a notebook or anything. Was that good or bad? And why was I worried about it?

"Destroyer suggested an illusion," I said. The idea was dismissed for the same reasons I gave him.

"We could set up a test, something only the killer would pass," D said. "It works because they are supposed to be here learning, right?"

"I thought maybe we could do a test too," Mark said. "Sort through charmed objects to find one that meant harm. We can use their belongings or something they've touched a lot."

"I will not allow magic used in such a way," Mrs. V said. "It steps very close to mind manipulation and would not work with the protector power."

We wouldn't know that until we tried, but I agreed with her. This was not going to be solved by magic. Or not in that way. "We have Magda's journal. Do the students know that? I can't remember."

"No. We only looked at it one time," Mrs. V said. She gave me one of her rare smiles. It was like facing a tiger just before the first bite.

"We let it slip, we create fake pages, see who tries to steal it."

20

The fake pages were looking good to me. We'd written things about each of the students that an empath might have concerns about. Mrs. V spelled my scrawl into Magda's neat script. Whoever broke into my office to read the evidence would believe it long enough for Mark to go in and arrest them. At least I hoped it was that simple.

"The suspects are conversing in the big room," Destroyer reported. "My spy does not believe they plan to move."

I loaded everything in my backpack and headed back to The Inner Spell with D at my side. Mark and Mrs. V would wait until we set the bait to arrive. Part of me was excited that we were about to catch our killer, the other part was terrified something would go wrong. I told the second part to buck up.

"Are you sure they'll hear us?" D asked.

"I'll make it happen," I said. "We need to see what's actually happening so I can improvise."

The ride wasn't hard or draining now that I'd done it a thousand times or more. We dropped the bikes in my parking lot and walked to the common room talking about nothing. Just general small talk. I noticed three squirrels and a small family of mice running into the cover of the closest trees.

"I have extracted my assets," Destroyer announced.

I wasn't the only one prepared for a disaster. Prepared was probably a bit optimistic.

Ravi, Jasper, and Samuel were in the common room, but not alone. Jeffery Peak sat with them, his leather jacket dropped over the back of a nearby chair.

"Ah, Cossi," he said as he stood to give me a hug. "We've been having a lovely discussion on the implications of change." He whispered in my ear. "Patience sent me an hour ago to keep them here."

Hearing Mrs. V's first name always made me want to laugh. I appreciated her forethought. Having a witch who looked like he'd ridden with The Hells Angels might keep things from going off the rails. "Maybe you should become one of my instructors."

"Ah, perhaps that would be a bigger commitment than I am ready for."

"I'll make tea," D said. "Then we can go up to your office."

My cue. I started talking as I walked over to join him. "Good. I'm not looking forward to reading what Magda wrote in her private journal."

I pulled it out and flipped through some pages. I couldn't risk checking to see which of my students paid more attention. I pretended to read a few passages and made a surprised noise.

We headed up to my suite without saying more. Jeffery called out his goodbye before we made it to the top of the stairs. So much for having some muscle.

"He is waiting in the tent," Destroyer said. "The ancient one will bring him back."

What the heck? Someone had been putting all kinds of things in place while we'd been on the road.

Step one complete, I left the journal open to one of our fake entries on my desk. D placed alarm wards on the door and the book. Now it was just a matter of giving an opportunity.

"How much is this affecting your training?" D asked. "We still need more protectors."

There wasn't much else to talk about. I hadn't put much energy into the longer term. "We're creeping along," I said. "But it's hard to pass on skills when I look at those three faces and know one of those witches killed Magda."

"We'll get them today," he said. "The killer won't be able to resist. If it was me, I might be curious, but I wouldn't break into your study. I'd be asking questions."

"I know. Mrs. V and I have to talk about the future. I don't have the brain space to do it now." I wished I could give a little push on the students, but that would muddy the proof.

"They are leaving the room," Destroyer said.

"I thought you sent your spies to safety." I told D what was happening.

"I am watching through the window." Destroyer sent me an image of the room. First time we'd shared visuals.

"Ravi is headed outside," I told D.

"He could still be the killer. Biding his time."

True. I watched through Destroyer's eyes, a weird, distorted view, as Samuel headed for the stairs, and Jasper followed him. One of them. It had to be. "We can go back in the building. I'd like to be closer when the ward alerts."

Ravi passed the tent and headed into the woods toward

the Earth Witch Village. As soon as he passed the first tree, D and I ran for the main building.

Destroyer left his perch on the windowsill and landed on my shoulder. I'd gotten used to the weight as he landed, and he'd learned to avoid piercing my skin. The common room was empty. A door closed upstairs without our alert. One of the suspects was in their room.

"There it is," D said.

A tingle run down my arm. The door to my suite was open.

D had set up a recording device so we could prove what happened. Magic was less reliable than plain technology in this case. We didn't have time to arrange a transmission so until we walked in, I had no idea who we'd find.

We reached the landing in a few seconds. The doors were closed; without the wards no one would know anything was wrong. I felt Mark and Mrs. V arrive. We were so close.

I stood back while Mark opened the door. Destroyer lifted off and flew through.

"Stop," Mark said in his cop voice.

I made it through the door to see Samuel with the journal in his hand. I rush of fury filled his aura, and he did nothing to cover it.

"You are under arrest for the murder of Magda Potter." Mark cast a restraint spell.

Mark and Mrs. V hurried to join us, and I heard Jasper's door open and close.

The space was too small for everyone to get inside. "The common room," I called out. "We'll bring him down."

Destroyer flew at Samuel and pooped on his head. "I will leave now. My spies will return."

I guess it meant something to crows, but I wouldn't let it

get in the way. I wasn't stupid enough to approach Samuel to clean up the mess, so I sent a spell his way. He could block it if he wanted to be stubborn, but that was up to him.

He inclined his head and let the spell work. It didn't stop at Destroyer's gift. When the spell was done, Samuel looked younger and his hair was black not blond. We'd been looking at an illusion the whole time.

21

As we watched the illusion slip away, more than just his age and hair changed. A look of confusion clouded his eye and his posture slumped.

"What's happening?" he asked. "Why am I here?"

It was a good try, but did he really expect the lies to past Mark and me? "Let's get downstairs where we have room to question him."

Mark nudged him and I saw his fingers toss a mute spell.

I sent a text to Jeffery to call the council together. Normally, we'd move him to Mark's house and into a cell, but I didn't want to move him. Too much chance to try an escape. He might not be able to get off the island, but there were too many places for him to hide. Tomorrow morning I was restarting the school, not participating in a manhunt.

Jeffery was already waiting when Mark and I escorted Samuel to the room. Ravi returned from his nightly walk as we arranged the chairs for the questioning. I asked him to bring Samuel down and join us. They were both affected by Magda's death, and by being suspects. This time the council wouldn't act in secret.

Mrs. V brought Tulip, Destroyer perched on a chair back; a memory of a courtroom drama came to me. "We'll start the questioning, and Jeffery will stand in for the council until they arrive. Please don't interrupt."

"Are we ready?" Mark asked. "I'll secure him to the chair before I remove the mute."

Suddenly I was supposed to lead the interrogation? This wasn't exclusively protector work, and I'd make sure that was understood after we were done. I wasn't training up replacements just so they could become the judicial arm of the magical world.

Mark settled him while Jeffery took a seat in the row of eight chairs for the council. Today I wasn't here as member. Mrs. V sat beside him, but Tulip stalked over to circle Samuel before flopping down in the back.

The council members drifted in, not all of them were near enough to arrive fast, but I was happier with more witnesses.

Dolph slid in next to Mrs. V and glared at me. "I have informed Lance his assistance is no longer needed. The camp is gone."

It felt like I was supposed to read something into that. Dolph and Lance were not exactly enemies, but they were rivals and mad enough at each other for it to it to be annoying.

"Let's get it over with," Mark said.

I walked to stand near Samuel who was now confined to a chair facing the audience. Despite the fact it must hurt, he was leaning forward and staring at the ground.

"You murdered Magda Potter. We will take anything you have to say to mitigate the punishment."

"I don't know what you mean," he said. "I remember

Magda, but the last thing I can recall is talking to your friend Zinnia. She must have done something to me."

His emotions didn't match the words. Far from being confused and recovering from a control spell, he was furious. Angry at himself for being caught so easily. Angry at me for... everything?

"You know I can read a lie," I said. "And Mark. Why are you continuing to pretend?"

Roy moved to stand beside me. "He smells of lies. Let me bite him."

"The dog has my permission," Destroy said.

"If biting is to be done, I will take the first turn," Tulip said.

I needed to put an end to the internal conversation. "The familiars are suggesting their own punishment. Samuel, your act is not fooling anyone."

He looked up at me. All presence was gone. His lips curled in a sneer and he laughed. "It was worth a try. I suppose I thought you were all stupid here."

No one gasped, but the tension ratcheted up a notch. He wasn't buying friends, or even a touch of sympathy.

"Why did you kill her?"

"We thought she was going to expose us," he spat the words. "She knew too much. You saw what she wrote."

My turn to be surprised. I checked with Destroyer. "Can we bring the journal here?"

Tulip stood and followed him out. "We cannot open your door."

I released the spell and felt the lock open. "Just nudge it."

"The council will review the book," I said. "The entries you tried to read were not Magda's. Did I accidentally hit on something when I faked them?"

Tulip returned with the journal in her mouth and dropped it at Mrs. V's feet.

"I didn't have time," Samuel said. "It doesn't matter. I'm not alone. The work will continue. No matter what you do to me."

He would tell us who was involved before we sent him away. He spoke the truth about not being alone.

"You didn't answer my question," I said. "I can force you, but I would prefer not to do that. Why did you kill her?"

"I told you she was going to expose us," he said.

"For what?" Mrs. V asked. "What have you done, or planned that would cause her death?"

I guess I was being too vague in my questions. Her words brought a cycle of anger and fear circling his emotions. The smooth shield was gone so if I needed to force the truth, it would be easy.

"Too much power is in the hands of too few people," he said. "Protectors are not our rulers. Too many decisions are made by people who don't care."

We didn't rule others. There was no ultimate authority in the magical world. Each community had a council. Solitary witches managed their own safety. "What makes you say that?"

"Tell me it's not true," Samuel said.

How was he able to slither out of answering? I wasn't using the protector power, but my own authority should be compelling.

"The protector asked you a question," Jasper shouted.

Samuel smirked. "So I should answer because of what she is? See? Too much power. She's not even lived among us for a year and she's a protector. Thank you for making my point."

"One more chance, before I show you what the protector can do." That sounded more threatening than I intended.

"You know I'm not a Whitlock," he said, his control slipping. "How do you think I was given to my new parents? People who shouldn't have had a child. People who neglected me?"

I almost took a step back to avoid being drowned in his tidal wave of pain and hatred. "Why would a protector be involved?"

"She was there when my parents died. She chose the Reese witches to raise me." The pain continued to pour out of him.

"I am sorry. Whoever this protector was, she wasn't acting officially." Handing a child to people who clearly didn't want children was about as far as you can get from protecting the magical world. It wasn't the time to explain that protectors were people. We weren't perfect. We made careless mistakes. It was time to name his allies.

As I opened my mouth to ask, I was pulled away. Tulip had my shirt in her teeth and was tugging me to the side. Roy barked, but I didn't understand any words, just danger.

Jasper was running to the front of the room.

Samuel was standing, his bonds broken.

I felt the power around me gathering to act, but it was too late.

Samuel grabbed Jasper and held a knife to his throat. "Time for me to leave, I think.

22

The shock stopped time.

The animals had known before me. How did Samuel hide such an action from me? I knew there was anger, but this? Sounds started to come back to me. It was only a second. Everyone was still in the same position.

Tulip let me go was a snarl that didn't translate to words. She stalked Samuel, but thank fate she didn't lunge at him. Jasper was too vulnerable for anyone to attack.

The witches drew around me. Dolph shifted to wolf form and joined Roy and Tulip to pace the pair, keeping Samuel from running. He might not have thought through how his hostage would slow his escape. Or he planned to use the knife and toss Jasper at us.

"You can't get away," I said. My voice sounded far more calm than I felt. I couldn't take my eyes off Samuel to take in everyone's position behind me. I relied on the waves of support.

"I am marshaling my forces," Destroyer said. "Hold him here until I am ready."

"I won't let him hurt Jasper," I thought back.

"We will see," he said. "Tulip is unconcerned with protecting your student. My wolves and eagles will do what they can. It is unfortunate that my bears are too far to join in."

If Samuel managed to slip outside, he would not survive. I didn't want the animals to kill him. I wanted him alive. We needed answers about his allies. We didn't need the stain our karma of his death. I'd been horrified when the German witches stripped the power from Sabine, but that seemed a kindness when it was done.

"Samuel, you won't get to leave the island. No one will take you back to the mainland. The animals are alert to find you. Let Jasper go and tell us who you worked with."

My protector power should be forcing him to comply by now. It was quiet. This incident didn't threaten our world. It was on me, Cossi Fortuna, to solve this. No. Not just me. I had the power of the council, and Mrs. V along with my friends and familiars to help.

"Cossi," D's voice cut in. "Lilibeth says the raptors have broken through her wards and are coming."

I wished I could answer him, or link him to Destroyer.

"They are coming to assist," Mrs. V said. "Tell her not to worry."

Of course, Tulip would tell her the plan.

"I don't need anyone's help," Samuel said. His superior attitude slipping. "I can find my way back. Boats are easy to steal."

The ward that kept the island invisible might block him from finding the mainland, or not.

"Why don't you tell us your plan. The reason you came here, the real one," Jeffery said. He pushed a spell of peace toward Samuel.

"Like some supervillain gloating while the hero builds a trap," Samuel shook his head. The movement caused the blade to inch closer to Jasper.

"Perhaps we'll understand," Mrs. V said. "This isn't the way to gain allies."

The questions gave me time to assess our moves. I was confident the others could keep Samuel talking. But they were waiting for me to stop this. Not just the witches, but Dolph, the familiars. The oncoming army of animals I could feel in my mind. And the earth witches, the solitaries... I had to stop him before a riot broke out. The overwhelming drive I felt coming from the entire island was revenge for threatening two protectors.

"You won't get to the boats," I said. "Let Jasper go. Talk to us. This doesn't have to be violent."

Jasper looked up at me. Then at his hands. He wasn't pleading for help. He was reminding me he was strong. A blacksmith.

"If you haven't stopped me by now, your protector power must be a myth."

I had other powers. He was right. I relied too much on being a protector. I wasn't in control and the longer it took, the worse it would get. I noticed a squirrel organizing mice next to the door. If the rodent unit of Destroyer's army ran up Samuel's body, Jasper might get away. But he might just lose his life.

"Everyone, stop." I kept my eyes on Samuel. Jasper would take his opportunity if I gave it.

"Let me go," Samuel said. "I'll release my hostage when I am away from you."

I sent a probe of power to him. It didn't go anywhere. Someone had warded Samuel with powerful spells.

I thought at Destroyer, "can you control the animals? To hold him, not harm?"

"Where's the fun in that?" He swooped to land on my shoulder.

"We need to have a talk about fun," I said. "Can you?"

"I will, but what is the value of taking this same situation outside. Here he is contained."

I told him my plan and he agreed.

"I will allow you to go, since you don't believe my warning. But you will release Jasper now."

He laughed. "Not likely. He's my only protection."

"I am giving you a choice," I said. "Not about freeing Jasper, but how easy it will be on you."

I flung my power around Jasper. He tensed but didn't struggle against the weight of it. Now Samuel wouldn't be able to budge from the spot unless he released his hostage.

"Nice, but would I trust you to let me leave?"

"You have my word. On my power," I said. "You will be allowed to exit this place without harm."

He glanced at the crowd of witnesses. The ones in my line of sight nodded.

"The lynx and the dog?"

"They are familiars. You know they are bound by their witches." I mean he didn't notice the mice or squirrel, so not my place to clarify.

I nudged his hope a little with my normal power. The protector still not weighing in.

He took a step away from Jasper.

When no one reacted. He lowered the knife and took another step.

Jasper swung a fist at Samuel's head, but he was already through the doorway.

23

His movement ignited the room with action. Destroyer, Tulip, and Roy raced after him. I ran to check Jasper. Dolph shifted back to human and everyone chased after Samuel.

Jasper assured me he was fine, if a little embarrassed at missing his punch. "It would have been over if just managed to connect."

Ravi rejoined us. "He didn't get far. This island is amazing. Everyone just works together without even talking about it."

I left Jasper and went to see if Destroyer's promise carried to his army. It did. And he was filling my head with his regal pride. Samuel was surrounded by wolves, actual not shifted ones. They looked hungry, but didn't wolves always look like they missed a few meals? Eagles perched on every surface they could find. The roof of the building, the tops of the tent braces, every chalet.

"Believe me now?" I asked. "You can't get away."

He blazed with anger. Whatever the reason he'd formed his alliance, it hadn't come from the adult we saw before us.

The hurt child radiated impotent fury. It was like a two-year-old having a tantrum. I couldn't be the only one who saw it.

"You swore on your power," he said betrayal hissing across the words. "Even a protector, maybe especially one, must abide by their oaths."

His arrogance was going to make everything worse for him—and us. "I swore you could exit, not escape. You still have a choice to tell us why. Give us something to help us show mercy."

He spun in the small circle the animals left him. It was odd that none of them showed anger. There was plenty of it coming from the people, but the animals were patient. When this was over, I'd find time to learn more about them. Being able to speak to animals—well, speak and understand any language to be specific, wasn't enough.

I'd get the next class going and then spend time on my own learning. But that was a sidetrack. This wouldn't be over until Samuel was in prison along with his allies.

"Why would you show me anything but control?" he asked. "We are not free as long as protectors decide our futures. I didn't want to be under your orders."

Wow, someone had taken him down a dark path. Then I checked myself. I didn't have any reason to think he was a victim. He took himself to this point. I scanned the power in the vicinity. Did he have an ally in the crowd? Someone confusing our logic?

No. It was him. Samuel had no shred of remorse or any desire to hear another view of the world. It was all someone else's fault.

"I don't know where you got your information, boy," Mrs. V said. "We protectors are not in control of anything. If we were, the world wouldn't need protecting, would it?"

He didn't answer. I was the only person he focused on, the others were what? Audience?

"Who else works with you?" I asked, pushing a little power at him. It flowed around the shield again. If I wanted to make him answer, I needed to push harder. It was too soon to risk the damage I might do.

As if he heard only half my thoughts, Samuel shook his head. "You would force me to betray my allies. Thank you for proving I am right."

An eagle lifted off from the first chalet roof and swooped over his head, one wing making contact with Samuel's arm. Not breaking it, but leaving a mark that would form a spectacular bruise.

"Keep them in control," I ordered Destroyer in my head.

"You said not to kill him," Destroyer responded.

"No hurting either. It gets in the way of convincing him we aren't planning something drastic."

He made a sound that I could only read as 'fine'. A few of the raptors flew away. The wolves remained. Samuel stood in a clear space circled by gray fur and sharp teeth.

I wouldn't apologize, but I didn't want him thinking I agreed the animals could harm him. "That should not have happened."

He rubbed at the wound. "Should or not, it did happen. I defied you and your minions attacked."

Minions? If only he knew the truth. But responding would only feed his beliefs. "It's your choice," I said. "Tell us who else is foolish enough to believe the same as you or wait until my protector power steps in. We will learn the names either way."

"He's up to something," Mrs. V said. "Take care."

What could he be up to? He had no path to escape. Even if he got away from us right now, we'd be able to find him.

"My pack is taking every boat from the island," Dolph said. "Swimming is not a good choice."

"Tulip tells me the eagles will pull you from the ocean much like a salmon is swept from a river," Mrs. V said. "Let us help you see the light."

If I had help with the questions, I could spare some attention to scan him, not probe, but his surface emotions would be enough. Instead of creating a spear, I formed a net of power. It settled on Samuel and fed me what he was feeling. Samuel didn't notice. He was repeating the same thing, maybe a few different ways. But he was stuck in a circle of you are evil as the questions came.

Confusion tainted his aura. Anger, no surprise. Fear. The one that grabbed my attention was glee. As I pulled my power to force my way through his shield, he acted.

Threads of power reached out to the witches closest to him. The ones aimed at me and Mrs. V withered, but Ravi was tangled in one magic, D in another.

I flung my hand out to sever the connections, but I was too late. Samuel drew out a portion of Ravi's environmental power and D's weather magic. Both sank to their knees.

A tornado scattered the guards. Birds flew out of danger, wolves raced to cover. Roy was blown aside as he tried to bite Samuel. Tulip leaped for him, but the wind forced her into the side of the tent.

I heard his laugh as Samuel dodged the spells cast to hold him—too late. Leaves, dust, and small pebbles rose to cover him as he ran to the forest.

24

I didn't wait for the others to react. A restraint spell wouldn't work unless I could see him. Roy and Dolph loped beside me as we passed the first few trees.

"Go ahead of me," I said. "Just be careful. We need him alive."

"Trees get in the way," Roy said. "Your familiar needs his birds looking."

Dolph didn't say anything. He was still a human even in wolf form, so carrying on a conversation in my head wasn't a possibility.

"Throwing spell," Destroyer said. "I will claim my due when he is punished. Birds cannot follow because of spells."

"We're on our own," I said as we crossed a small brook. I could hear others coming behind us. Too much noise. Tracking him by the sound of his movements wouldn't work. He could have gone down or upstream. Either way would lead him farther into the dense growth.

"I've called the shifters to join the search," Dolph said shifting to human. Naked human. I handed him my scarf. He didn't care about displaying his body, I found it distracting. "I think our best shot is to figure out what a city witch might think is the safe move."

"Any guesses?" Yes, I qualified as a city witch, but I'd adapted to living on Henbane.

"He crossed the stream," Roy said. "Shifter is correct. Only a city dweller would miss the opportunity to break his scent."

I passed on the news to Dolph. "We can follow Roy, but I'd rather not lag behind."

Dolph was sniffing the air. He stared at Roy like they could talk. As far as I knew it wasn't possible. "If he's fighting the birds, we may not have a choice. We wait and send people in different directions, or we follow. He doesn't have much of a lead."

I was not waiting. We were already past the brook and following Roy on the trail. I couldn't risk delaying to talk strategy. "The birds don't need to track him," I said almost to myself as an idea formed. "But Destroyer's spies have been watching for days."

I thought at my familiar. "Where has Samuel been on his walks? Maybe he was scouting his escape route?"

"Shall I send you the answers, or just the result?" Destroyer asked.

No pomp or imperial nonsense. He was on the hunt. "The results, unless you think we need to change direction."

We kept moving while my familiar gathered the data. How was Samuel staying so far ahead of us? I had a dog used to hunting and a shifter with me, and the fallen trunks and dense bushes were slowing us down. Upside, I wasn't out of breath.

"Any signs he's pass through here?"

"No," Dolph said. "That's worrying because it is far

easier to set a false trial with your scent than to move rapidly through the forest without leaving a mark."

"Not false trail," Roy told me.

I passed that on and then Destroyer interrupted. "Earth witch village and to the edges of the trees. Did not meet with anyone."

"The edges of the trees?" Dolph said. "Like the cliffs? Hmm. I suppose it's comforting to know his accomplice is not here on Henbane."

To be here, it meant our wards were not working properly. The accomplice would have been here before, or been brought by someone. Without Mark knowing. Now my protector power twitched into wakefulness.

"I don't know what it means," I said. "If Samuel didn't violate our wards, why am I suddenly flooded with protector power?"

Dolph looked at me before lifting me over a huge trunk. "Why would I know that? Does it matter? When we catch him, Samuel will be forced to speak."

There was absolutely no guarantee that the power would be active at that point. Perhaps Samuel was doing harm to the island right now.

"I have heard from my ground forces that your target is running toward the angry water."

I felt the surprise that a mouse or something had outsmarted his birds.

"How far?" I asked.

"You know they are bad at distances. I will ask some gulls. It may take time to get sense from them. Continue on your path."

I couldn't wait for my familiar to get gulls to think beyond food. "He's heading for the cliffs," I said aloud. "How far can he be?"

"We're almost there," Dolph said. "Slow down, I don't want us to stumble into something risky."

The whole protect the protector thing. His attitude was very different from when I first arrived. He hadn't wanted me to stay. I didn't react to the alpha energy, but it wasn't the time to fight that battle.

Roy slowed as the trees thinned. He went into a low crawl and then came to a halt. "On the edge. Waving to someone high."

"A helicopter?" I joined Dolph behind the last tree. "Would that work? Please say no."

"I don't hear anything," he answered. "But with a tracker and a very trusting pilot, maybe. They would need to navigate without paying heed to what they see, or what they don't see. Very dangerous."

That explained the protector power.

We glanced around the trunk of our hiding place. Samuel was standing at the edge of the cliff, waving his arms like one of those guys at the airport guiding a plane in. Dolph's shifter hearing wouldn't be fooled. And the number of birds filling the air above our fugitive would crash any helicopter trying to land.

I felt the protector power recede, but not go back to sleep. The magic world was still in danger.

"How do we bring him back from the edge?"

"He's distracted," Dolph said. "I can try alpha setting."

While it worked to lead his shifters, I'd already experienced how a witch felt. Yes, we could ignore him, but it took some will. Samuel's focus on his rescue might not notice.

I nodded to give him the okay.

"Move to the center of the clearing."

I almost started walking myself.

Samuel turned and followed the compulsion. I saw the

moment that he realized. Too bad for him that an Australian cattle dog, and shifter had different ideas.

Roy nipped his heels and Dolph's wolf pushed Samuel face down on the flat rocks.

I put a restraint spell on him again. Dolph searched his pockets and found the charms he'd used to break the last one.

By the time he was standing and waiting to be escorted to jail for more questioning, the remaining witches broke through the trees.

Destroyer landed on my shoulder almost knocking me down in shock.

"I order you to avoid that much danger in the future."

"I'll do my best."

25

A big part of me had been disappointed when I learned there was no transportation spell. I mean, wouldn't that be great? As we headed back to the village and Mark's house, my body caught up with all the scratches and bumps that I'd accumulated on the run to catch our killer.

The animals told me about a shortcut before disappearing. I thanked them all for their help and instructed everyone to follow Roy who said he knew the route.

Now we were standing in the crowded hall outside the jail cell. Mark reinforced the security wards and Samuel sat on a bench with his wrists in cuffs set far enough apart that he couldn't pick the locks, or cast a spell.

"Roy will watch," Mark said. "We all need a respite. Clean up, deal with your wounds and come back in half an hour."

The order didn't apply to me or D. He showed us to the two en suite bathrooms. Mrs. V, who was surprisingly untouched by the chase, handed us both salves.

"Be fast," she said. "I don't trust that witch to cooperate.

Mark and I will guard him. Then he can clean up while you and D take over."

She wasn't the only one afraid that Samuel would find another way to escape. A shower would be wonderful and not just for the physical cleaning. I grabbed a cloth and ran it under the tap, and I added a little cleaning power, just to get rid of any infection that might lurk in the scrapes.

I was clean in about thirty seconds. The salve took another half minute. Then I marched back to stand watch with Mrs. V. Two protectors should be able to contain him.

"Why give a half hour to everyone?" I asked when we were alone.

She looked at me with the familiar expression of 'why do you need to ask'.

I thought through the implications. "My protector power is still waiting. So there's still a danger to the world. I guess now we have him, we can take a beat. But his partner or gang is still free."

She nodded, keeping her eyes on Samuel. He didn't look up.

"Everyone was angry and exhausted," I said again, wishing I'd taken a moment to read the emotions at the cliff. "Clear heads. They need to get their anger under control. We might end up making things worse if the emotions are too high."

"Yes. You do really need to have confidence that you know the answers before you ask." She shifted her gaze back to me. "Did you notice when I stopped answering? When it thought you were ready to be on your own?"

My first instinct was to say no. But that was as bad as automatically asking rather than thinking. "Germany. From the moment we got the call from Grete. I was so wound up about leaving everyone here that I didn't notice." I searched my memory for our conversations about setting up the training. Yes, she'd given input, but I couldn't remember a situation where she answered a question on a topic other than her opinion.

"You are sneaky," I said. "When this is done, we need to talk about the school."

"We do. But let's get through this first."

D joined us as set up to record the interrogation. Both with recall spells and a mundane recording app on his phone. "I'll go help Mark get the chairs."

The last time we'd taken part in questioning a prisoner here, Lance, Lilibeth, and I were relegated to the back and standing on chairs was the only way to see. Now I was a protector, so I'd be in the front, but D would be in the back, because his dad was in residence so didn't need a representative.

The council members drifted in, none of them needing thirty minutes to prepare. Mark stood before the bars of the cell.

"Samuel Whitlock, you are charged with the death of Magda Potter. Other charges will come from the protectors. If you choose to answer questions fully and honestly, it may go in your favor."

The prisoner nodded. I didn't feel any lies, but he hadn't said he agreed. The nod could have been acknowledgment that he'd heard.

"Are you ready to confess? To provide a reason?" Mark asked.

I'd expected a series of specific questions, but we'd learned from Phillip's hexes that caution was a good starting place. Every time one of the hexed witches tried to tell us the truth, they'd died.

"She knew too much. Yes, I killed her. She knew who I was. I changed my name. I was born Samuel Reese."

Was that too easy? He'd fought us every step to this point.

"The cell is reinforced with spells to compel the truth," Mrs. V said. "And two protectors might make a difference. I told Mark to ask broad questions."

Hmm, I didn't even have to ask.

"Why change your name?" Mark asked.

"I was no one. When people thought I was a Whitlock, they treated me different."

"You have your confession," Jeffery said. "I speak for the council when I say, it's time to hear about his allies."

That meant me or Mrs. V. I didn't wait for her to nudge me.

"You have put our world at risk," I said. "By forming an alliance to attack the protector school, you risk exposure. Why did you do that?"

He glared at me and pressed his lips together.

"It would be better if you told her," Mrs. V said. "We can make you answer."

He continued his battle to stop any words coming out.

"Who are your allies?" I didn't like using the compulsion, so I was giving him more chances than Mrs. V might have.

He shook his head and pulled on his restraints.

My protector power twitched to let me know it was time.

"One more chance before I force the truth. Why threaten our safety and who helped you?"

He tried to stand, but the cuffs pulled on him to keep Samuel in the chair.

Then something broke through his shield. And he sobbed.

"Tell her," Mark said.

"I did already. A protector gave me to witches who didn't care. Isn't that enough?"

Yes, he'd told us his story and that he'd changed his name, but it could all have been a lie. Now that story was confirmed we could move on.

"I am sorry that happened," I said. "Who helped you?"

The hatred that blazed from him made me take a step back. I would find that protector and ask what the heck they were doing to damage a child so much he'd expose our world.

"One witch. No gang." Each word was forced through clenched teeth.

My power surrounded him. He had no choice but to answer truthfully and fully. I needed the right questions, but a name would get us started.

"Who?" I felt the pulse of my power.

"Darla Goodmother." He fought my power and his restraints.

"Stop resisting," I said. "You have no options. A broken arm or two won't kill you but the pain will make you regret the fight."

My perception extended around the room. I heard Mark calling someone to take Darla into custody. I felt Mrs. V's approval. The council's impatience. My friend's surprise.

"What was your goal?" The question came from the magic, not me.

He sobbed and then let the tension in his body go. "I didn't want to expose our world. Who would bring that on? I wanted the protectors to know what they'd done."

My protector power withdrew and suddenly I was just Cossi Fortuna.

"You will be transported tonight to serve your life in our prison," Mark said. "Your accomplice will join you."

Two weeks later I sat in my suite at the Inner Spell with all the notes and decisions we'd made about the training scattered around me. Mrs. V was on her way, and I still didn't have any idea what we needed to do to improve the sessions. Ravi and Jasper were gone, with a promise of a place in the next session if they wanted it.

Even the few lessons we'd managed made a difference. Ravi's passion for the environment was smoothed enough that he might make a real change for the better. Jasper was on the way to healing the pain of his grief and arriving at the point where he could function—no one ever managed to get over the death of a loved one.

Samuel's co-conspirator had a similar story about a protector when they caught her.

Destroyer was off doing something imperial with his subjects. I was surprised at how he'd marshaled what I'd thought of as a fantasy. I still didn't know if the idea of a united animal empire was a good thing.

Tonight, Lance, Mark, D, and Lilibeth were coming to stay over with food and drink from Sheena's bar. We needed some reconnecting as friends time. Lilibeth had announced a change in her desire to be a detective. She still didn't want to do it, but as she put it, *I didn't mean for you to cut me out. I need the gossip.*

So, Mrs. V and I had hours to figure out our next step. I hoped she had some ideas. And that she'd tell me what they were.

I put the kettle on in my small kitchen when I heard the first step on the stairs.

By the time Mrs. V walked through my door, two mugs and a plate of Valerie's ginger cookies were on the table.

"This place looks like a tornado," she said. "Does that mean you've been assessing the situation?"

"Not successfully, but I've tried meditation, reading the notes online, printing them out and grouping them. Creating a spreadsheet of important points. A spell to raise meaning."

I poured the tea and passed her my jar of honey.

"We certainly did our best," she said. "Continuing to improve that plan may not be our way forward."

I'd come to that conclusion about an hour ago. "Yeah, I kept looking for flaws and opportunities based on a failed project. We need to start from scratch, right?"

She sipped her tea and ate a cookie while she considered. In the past I would have interpreted it as her waiting for me to catch up, but not this time. She didn't have a concrete plan.

When she washed the last crumb down with her tea, she waved her hand. The mess of pages and sticky notes flew into piles. "That will make them easier to compost. Now we have learned a few lessons. First step is to define scratch, yes?"

The logic was sound. But how different could the meanings be? We needed to create protectors.

"I say the beginning was realizing roles could be taught," I said.

"I agree that might be the start, but I would go back further. When protector numbers declined. That Samuel made one very good point. Why did we ignore what the universe, or whatever, wanted? Fewer protectors might mean we don't need them. And I see two reasons. One, the chances of us being exposed was exceedingly low, or critically high."

Protector power flooded both of us. It approved, but with what? How could high-risk equal fewer protectors?

"The other question I have is why did we think I could do it? We have actual universities. Experts in teaching. We could have been consultants."

She nodded and reached for another cookie. This time her pause was definitely giving me time to process.

We'd jumped into this academy without looking for options. I didn't think either of us did it because we didn't trust anyone. The power didn't stop us, so it wasn't a risk. We caught a potential huge problem before it grew.

"If we didn't hold the first lessons," I said. "Samuel might have created a larger group of conspirators. So, our job was to weed the two witches out. Both Jasper and Ravi had potential to escalate until our world was exposed. Accident or on purpose, the end result is the same. Does the protector power use us, or do we use it?'

She pushed the plate of cookies toward me and nodded at my tea. "You need sugar. I can't answer most of that, but I'd say a little of both. We learned of threats we might have missed until they got too big. I'd like to think we use the power and it uses us. What do you think our next step is?"

The big question. I set a spell to warm my tea and nibbled the treat while I thought. The bite of the ginger settled my thoughts.

"There are two directions," I said. "We need to hand off the training of protector candidates to a qualified school. And we need to assess the remaining protectors. Whoever interfered with Samuel and Darla's fate created problems. I didn't think social work was part of our job. Maybe instead of training, we should build some... rules? Guidelines?"

Before she answered a bloom of heat rose in my chest. Then another. I looked at Mrs. V and saw the same in her aura, not just heat, sparkles.

"One of those is true," she said, a real smile on her face. "Two new protectors have found their purpose. Our job is your second idea."

WANT MORE

Ready for your next Henbane adventure?

Protector numbers are increasing. The school project is closed, Cossi has time to work on her skills. Well, until a body turns up and she's on the hunt for a killer again.

REVIEW

If you enjoyed reading A Cursed Course please consider helping other readers to find the story by using the QR code to leave a review.

FREE BOOK

Use the QR code to Claim your copy of Magic Will Out when you sign up for my newsletter and follow Cossi as she seeks answers to her past.

ALSO BY POPPY

For more books by Poppy Bridgeman

scan the QR code below.

ABOUT POPPY BRIDGEMAN

Hi, I'm Poppy Bridgeman, the cozy mystery alter ego of Canadian author P A Wilson. Poppy was "born" because sometimes stories need a gentler touch—with a little magic, a dash of humor, and plenty of sleuthing spirit.

As Poppy, I write the *Witch of Henbane Island* series (where witches and festivals collide with mysteries), the *EB Eats Culinary Mysteries* (a small-town diner, a determined heroine, and murder on the menu), and the *Pages & Paws Bookstore Mysteries* (a Devon bookshop, two mischievous corgis, and plenty of secrets tucked between the shelves).

When I'm not tangled in my characters' escapades, I'm happily tangled in yarn—I knit, weave, and doodle in sketchbooks between writing sessions. I also love to travel, finding inspiration for charming settings, quirky characters, and suspicious strangers wherever I go.

Home base is the Vancouver area, where I juggle writing as both Poppy and P A Wilson. Whichever name is on the cover, I'm always chasing the next story.

ACKNOWLEDGMENTS

Writing may look like a solitary pursuit, but I could never do this alone. I've been lucky to have support, encouragement, and inspiration from so many corners that it's impossible to thank everyone properly—but I'll try.

My writing groups keep me sharp and creative: The Vancouver Writers Social Group challenges me to see stories in new ways, The Royal City Literary Arts Society has given me the chance to learn from generous and talented writers, and The Other 11 Months group reminds me that words on the page are what really matter. My critique partners, with their sharp eyes and honest feedback, make sure each story is the best version it can be.

And of course, my heartfelt thanks to my beta readers. You catch the wobbly bits, cheer for the good ones, and remind me that these stories aren't just mine—they're meant for you, my readers.